"Congratulations, Mason. You're a dad."

Mason was about to grunt a reply when his brother continued. "A bachelor dad, of course. A single father. An unwedded man."

"Thank you, Last. You can go now."

Last turned serious. "Mason, it couldn't have happened to a nicer guy. Just be nice to Mimi, okay? That's your future lying in there next to the little pink giraffe. You don't want to goof up the thing that means the most to you."

Last thundered down the stairs and went out the front door. Mason sighed, taking one last look at his daughter, then headed toward his own room.

Last was right about one thing. Nanette was his future. However, he would allow Mimi to visit whenever she wanted. Underneath his anger, he didn't really intend to keep her away from her child. As long as everything went his way.

As long as Nanette stayed here with him, where she belonged.

Dear Reader,

The wild boys of Malfunction Junction meant so much to me to write, and I greatly appreciate the love and enthusiasm you have shown for the wily Jefferson brothers. They are a tightly knit family who tried to do right, and now they have their own happy ending. I lived with these brothers for three years, and am delighted that you took them into your hearts, as well. My mother, sister and grandmother were not able to read any of the series, so I was fortunate to have you to love the stories, which were very much a part of my heart. Your letters meant a lot.

It's always hard to say goodbye, but through the blessings of fate it turns out we are saying goodbye only temporarily. In *Crockett's Seduction* we met a trio of determined ladies who happened upon Valentine's special Men Only Day. These women have a very stubborn sheriff back in their small town—and some tricky characters to outwit—so they are taking some of the good ideas they learned in Union Junction back to their tiny town of Tulips, Texas. Please join me in the next chapter of fun as the Forrester family learns that tea at the Tulips Saloon is anything but sanely predictable, and Ladies Only Day is introduced in a town where men think they are in charge.

Best wishes and much love,

Tina Leonard

P.S. Please visit me at my Web site www.TinaLeonard.com.

MASON'S MARRIAGE
Tina Leonard

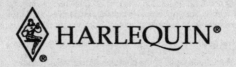

TORONTO • NEW YORK • LONDON
AMSTERDAM • PARIS • SYDNEY • HAMBURG
STOCKHOLM • ATHENS • TOKYO • MILAN • MADRID
PRAGUE • WARSAW • BUDAPEST • AUCKLAND

ISBN 0-373-75117-6

MASON'S MARRIAGE

Copyright © 2006 by Tina Leonard.

This edition published by arrangement with Harlequin Books S.A.

® and TM are trademarks of the publisher. Trademarks indicated with ® are registered in the United States Patent and Trademark Office, the Canadian Trade Marks Office and in other countries.

www.eHarlequin.com

Printed in U.S.A.

To the readers who have loved the
Cowboys by the Dozen—every one of these
stubborn Malfunction Junction men—
thank you with all my heart.

Books by Tina Leonard

HARLEQUIN AMERICAN ROMANCE

*Cowboys by the Dozen

Prologue

I was sure as hell no hero. I don't know why
she loved me. But she did, and I loved her for
it, with all the love a man can give anyone.
—*Maverick Jefferson, from a notation in his*
private journal, which was delivered to his son
Mason by family friends.

Mimi Cannady took a deep breath as the election
results came in. Of course, there had never been any
doubt that Mason Jefferson, popular cowboy and
owner of Union Junction Ranch, affectionately
known in these parts as Malfunction Junction, would
be elected sheriff by a landslide. The only doubt
she'd had recently was when she would tell Mason
the truth about his daughter.

Mason came to stand beside her, after everyone

had finished congratulating him and filed out. "Thanks for all your hard work on the campaign, Mimi. Although I'm not sure what kind of adventure you've gotten me into this time."

Knowing now, when he was happily elected, was probably the perfect time for the truth, she smiled wanly. "Mason, I have to talk to you about something."

"I'm listening," he said. "What does my campaign manager want to tell me?"

Mimi tried to stop her hands from shaking, but she couldn't. She willed her heart to be brave and told her spirit that she had faced more difficult challenges.

Friendship was really all she'd ever had from Mason Jefferson—and she'd desperately tried to hang on to it over the years. But she knew hanging on to Mason's goodwill was selfish when she thought about what her daughter and Mason were missing by not knowing their true relationship.

"Mason," she said softly. "Maybe I've waited too long to tell you this, but there's something you must know. I hope you can forgive me for not telling you sooner." Taking a deep breath, she forced herself to speak. "Nanette is your daughter."

The victory smile he'd been wearing faded from his face. He stared at her, clearly dumbfounded. "Of course she is," he said. "I mean, I love her as if she were my very own flesh and blood."

Mimi's heart thudded low and slow, heavy and hard and almost painful. "Mason, the night before I got married—"

"Don't say another word," Mason commanded, his voice like cold, hard marble. He stared at her, obviously remembering that night, and suddenly looking like a complete stranger she didn't know at all. The longest seconds of her life passed as he studied her face, his gaze hawkish and suspicious. She could almost hear a door slam shut between them.

He strode from the campaign "war room." Mimi hurried after him, but Mason turned, holding up a hand so that she wouldn't follow. Helplessly, she watched as he went to Widow Fancy, who kept the town paperwork records, and whispered something in her ear.

The two of them walked down the hall of the old courthouse and into the records room. A loud click erupted as Mason locked the door behind them. Realizing what he was about to do, Mimi ran to bang on the door.

"Mason! Let me in!"

But there was no reply.

Chapter One

There were many important memories in Mason Jefferson's life, some so poignant that they were etched like sand-scratched glass in his mind. One was realizing his father had gone away, leaving him in charge of a family of rambunctious, grieving boys. That was the moment Mason had first learned the meaning of the word *responsible*.

After that, he'd been responsible for a hell of a lot. It wasn't easy being a parent when all he'd known how to be was a boy.

Another sharp memory was the day Mimi had gotten married. Right up until the moment she'd said "I do," he'd believed she would not marry another man. He'd had every right to think that, since just the night before he had made wild, uninhibited love with her. It was the only time in his life he could truly say he'd let loose the mantle of responsibility that he'd worn over the years—and he'd loved every sweet moment of it.

"May God forgive me," he muttered to himself as he sat in a hard-backed wooden chair, one of the pieces of furniture that came with the sheriff's office. "May God forgive me for the sin of loving another man's wife."

But there was no forgiveness for that, which he knew too well by now. The price to pay for stealing forbidden love was that you paid forever. He'd paid every time he'd seen Mimi, every holiday, every waking moment of his life.

The price was never enough to stop a man from the folly of his ways. Love would not stop just because a man knew the price was out of his reach.

Mason crossed his ankles and rested his boots on the old, well-worn desk that had belonged to Mimi's father, the former sheriff, Sheriff Cannady. This was his office, and it would take a long time for Mason to be able to believe the truth of the bronze door placard that read Sheriff Mason Jefferson.

In contrast to the office, the sign was bright and shiny, with its black letters stern against the bronze. So official. So steeped with responsibility. He had the sheriff's office, and his chair, and his desk. But he did not have the sheriff's daughter.

And now, whether he liked it or not, the final price to pay for all he'd been given, for all he'd pushed aside to be with Mimi that one night, was learning that Nanette was his daughter. Mason sighed, and stared at the ceiling, barely noticing the new coat of paint.

He remembered the day Nanette had been born. He'd helped deliver her, his own hands trembling with amazement as he'd held her. Stubborn Mimi had refused to leave her very ill father to go to a hospital, and her husband, Brian Flannigan, had been working in Houston or Austin or somewhere. Mason had stepped in, the mantle of responsibility heavy on his shoulders, to help Mimi, though the biggest part of his heart was fiercely glad that he'd gotten to share that moment with the woman he cared so much about.

The baby had let out a fierce wail of welcome to her new world, and the sound was another sharp-scratched memory he would never forget—God's miracle writhing between his big palms. Mason had shaken a mental fist at the price he would pay for being unrepentantly glad that it was he in that room and not Brian.

He had never cared about mental costs, anyway. If he had one goal in life that he would never speak aloud—not to his youngest brother, Last, not to anyone, not even Mimi—it was that he would never, ever crack as his father had.

"Damn it," he whispered under his breath. "*I* will never leave anything behind that I love."

In spite of the anger and too-deep sense of betrayal he felt for Mimi now, Nanette was never going to think that her father had left her behind. It was his solemn vow. For stealing forbidden love, he was willing to pay the price forever.

Mimi was just going to have to deal with that.

THERE WAS NOTHING HEROIC about a man who decided that he would be a father to his child, no matter what, Mimi decided, watching Mason pack up Nanette's things.

"Mason," she said, "you're being an ass. You cannot take my daughter and move her out to Malfunction Junction."

Mason didn't stop folding Nanette's clothes as he put them methodically in her little pink suitcase.

"Mason!" Mimi reached out to take the suitcase away from him. *"No."*

Silently, he looked up and met her eyes. His gaze was so flat and devoid of the friendship they'd once shared that Mimi released the suitcase when he put his hand on it.

This was not the result she'd envisioned when she'd confessed her secret, and her heart was completely broken. Not only had she lost Mason, who was her best friend and the man she'd loved all her life, but he seemed determined to take the one fragment of her world that she'd hung on to with gratitude and wonder. Nanette was her salvation, her dream come true, her only piece of Mason—Mimi had accepted that there would be no more than the child of their one stolen night.

"Mason, please," she said. "You know a child needs its mother. Nanette won't understand."

He snapped the suitcase shut. "Nanette would understand even less a father who didn't put her first in his life. She belongs on my ranch, and that's where she's going to live." His tone had flattened out, and now he picked Nanette up in his big arms. "A father puts his family in front of everything else on the planet. And if you don't agree, ask your father if he was putting you first all the years he raised you after your mother left."

She stepped back from his words. "Mason, it's not the same thing!"

He walked out the door and her words fell unheeded. Over his shoulder, Nanette looked at her with big eyes, completely satisfied to rest her chin on her father's shoulder and go with him. And why shouldn't she? All she'd ever known was that Uncle Mason was one of the three people who loved her most: her mother, her grandfather and her uncle Mason.

Only Uncle Mason was really her father, and it was time Nanette knew it. Mimi blinked back fast tears and resisted the urge to run after Mason. He couldn't just take his child, Mimi thought wildly. But who would stop him? He was Nanette's father, he was completely within his rights to at least partial custody and he was the sheriff.

A growing sense of desperation filled her, tightening her stomach. She ran out the front door to his truck as he switched on the engine. The truck window was open and she put imploring fingers on Mason's strong chest. "Mason, I'm coming, too! Don't rip us apart!"

He removed her fingers and shook his head. "You've done enough, Mimi. Some space between me and you is what is badly needed."

He drove off, leaving Mimi stunned. Watching the truck pull away felt like a slow-motion tragedy from a movie. Her breath caught in her throat and her chest cramped, hurting more than anything she had ever felt. It was her heart, she was certain it was. Two of the three people she loved most on the planet had just left her, and the pain was more than she could bear.

She sank to her knees. Yes, she'd made the wrong choice. She'd lied. But she couldn't believe that the man she'd grown up with had turned away from her in her hour of greatest need.

Chapter Two

Somehow Mimi made it through the night, but by the next day, she knew she was going to need help getting through to Mason. He wouldn't answer either the house phone or his cell phone. She was growing desperate. How long did he intend to keep their child away from her?

"Dad," Mimi said, striding into the living room where her father sat playing cards with Barley, Calhoun Jefferson's father-in-law. Calhoun was one of Mason's younger brothers, and he was crazy in love with his wife, Olivia, as she was with him. "When you have some time, I really need to talk to you."

Barley stood. "Good. I'm going to Baked Valentines to get a box of cookies, Sheriff. Me and you are going to go hit some skeets and snack on some chocolate chips."

When her father had fallen ill with liver disease, Mimi had spent a hellish year thinking she was going to lose him. But he'd recovered miraculously, thanks in part to the scrawny rodeo clown who spent so much time dragging the sheriff to social events. But skeets weren't a social occasion that required chocolate chip cookies, since skeets weren't real birds.

"I don't remember skeets liking cookies from Baked Valentines," she said.

Barley laughed and waved goodbye. "Be back in a bit."

"He's crazy," her father said happily. "He's determined to fix me up with Widow Fancy, so we're going over there tonight."

Mimi blinked. "Widow Fancy? I had no idea you—"

"No. Now don't you get started on that." The sheriff chuckled. "Barley's just stirring things up. I'm fine the way things are. I've got you and my granddaughter, and that's all I need." He walked into the kitchen, taking out a big pot. "But I am going to make some soup to freeze for winter. Widow Fancy gave me a recipe." He grinned. "Think I can make the base for tortilla soup?"

"Yes," Mimi said, amazed that her father was apparently taking up cooking lessons from the widow.

"Now, what's on your mind? Tell me while you chop some poblanos for me. Got them fresh the other day, and they are hot!" He looked around. "Nanette gone to Mason's? Or Olivia's?"

Mimi told the tears rimming the sides of her eyes to go away, and when they wouldn't, she wiped them.

"Hay fever?" her dad asked.

"I told Mason the truth," Mimi said.

The sheriff stopped, turning to give her his full attention. "The truth?"

"About Nanette."

Her father frowned. "What truth?"

Mimi sank into a chair, her legs no longer holding her. "Dad, I've made a big, really awful mess."

He sat across from her, his face etched with concern. "There's nothing that can't be fixed."

"This cannot be fixed." She took a deep breath, gazing toward the ceiling for a few moments. "No one knows this except Bandera and Holly. And Brian. I mean, of course Brian always knew. Bandera...I don't know why I told him. The guilt was beginning to eat at me. Or maybe it wasn't guilt. Conscience. Was I right, or wrong?"

"Honey, you're not making any sense."

"Dad," Mimi said, desperate to sort her emotions, "Mason is Nanette's father. Not Brian."

Her father blinked. "Mason?"

"Yes," Mimi said, feeling shame and embarrassment sweep over her. "Oh, God."

"And Brian knows."

"Yes."

"That's why the two of you didn't stay married."

"Well," Mimi said miserably, "we never planned to stay together. I got married so that you would know I was happy in my life. I thought you were going to die, and I wanted you to see me settled with a good man and security." She breathed deeply, though it never felt as though her lungs fully expanded. "I wanted you to have a grandchild before you passed away. We just wanted you to be happy. Both of us did." She wiped errant tears away.

"So you two were never...husband and wife."

"No."

"It was never a true marriage, but somehow there is Nanette."

"The night before," Mimi whispered.

"Yegods," her father said. "Mimi, I do not want to know one more thing than what you just told me." He leaned back in the chair, staring at her. "Damn it, I do! Mimi, if you and Mason were together the night before your wedding, why didn't you just...call the whole damn thing off?"

"I couldn't!" Mimi jumped to her feet. "What would it have changed, Dad? Mason wasn't going to walk with me down the aisle! I could have spent the rest of my life loving him, and it wouldn't have made a bit of difference. And at that point, I had you to think about! How many years did you think of me first before yourself, Dad, after Mom left?" She shook her head, her tears too great to keep back. "I was determined that you leave the earth knowing I was happy if it was the last thing I did. And I did it."

"Yes, you did." Her father rubbed at his chin. "And that baby brought me right back, I'll admit. Brought out the fighting spirit in me. But, Mimi," he said, his tone still surprised, "what does Mason say now?"

"Mason is a miserable mule." Mimi tore at her eyes with a piece of tissue, swiping away the water but not the pain. That would never go away. "He took Nanette."

A frown crossed her father's face. "Took her?"

"To live with him. For good." Mimi sat again, feeling faint. "He said that a child needed its father."

"And its mother, when matters work out best," her father said.

"I don't feel any differently than he does," Mimi said, recognizing a trace of bitterness in her own voice. "I know the pain of abandonment. I would never allow Nanette to grow up without her mother."

"I'm sure Mason isn't thinking clearly right now," he said, "but you two need to talk."

Mimi shook her head. "He's not in the mood to talk to me."

"I don't care about moods. I care about Nanette." Her father patted her hand. "She's blessed, you know. She has two parents to love and care about her, even if they neither one think straight all the time. Surely it's not as bleak as it seems, honey."

"It feels horrible."

"Mason wasn't walking out on *you*," her father said. "It's really all about his child."

"What does that mean?" Mimi asked. "I should stop loving Mason? Or be glad that he's so stubborn about being with Nanette?"

"Maybe yes, maybe no. But you've got two different emotional paths warring inside you, Mimi, and that's no way to help yourself. Or Nanette. Decide if you want to fight for your daughter, or fight for Mason. Because right now your heart is breaking two ways." He rubbed her cheek and touched her hair. "I'm sorry I made you feel that you had to take care of me."

"Oh, Dad," Mimi said, taking his hand in hers to rest against her cheek. "I'm never going to apologize for loving Mason, and I'm never going to be anything but deliriously happy that Nanette is my daughter. You got well. Brian married his girlfriend. Somehow I thought everything would work out...."

Mimi lowered her head. And that was when she realized what she'd really thought would work out, her deepest secret: she'd been waiting for Mason.

She was his for the taking, and she always had been.

MASON LOOKED DOWN at his daughter as she lay sleeping in the guest room, which would now need to be converted into Nanette's bedroom. He felt a sense of excitement at the thought and an over-whelming need to catch up in her life. How did he tell this child that he was her father and not her beloved uncle? When should he tell her?

When I have completely absorbed it myself. And that was going to take some time. But he missed the moments when she might have called him Dad or Father. Daddy. Many of his brothers had children, or had them on the way. He'd never known when or with whom he'd have children.

Maybe because he'd always been waiting on... something. He didn't know what. Impatiently, he brushed away those wistful thoughts and focused solely on the child sleeping soundly in front of him.

My daughter. My child. My very own.

It was a heady thought, even more wildly satisfying than staying on the meanest bull, or being elected sheriff, or anything in his life, for that matter. He'd done a lot of good things, and some not so admirable, but this…this child was as near to an angel as he figured anyone could be.

He had to tell his brothers, when the time was right. He went to sink into a rocking chair so he could sit and watch Nanette sleep, and as he sat, the terrible thought hit him that maybe his brothers already knew.

Last, for example, had looked at him strangely once when Mason had told Nanette that one day he wanted a little girl just like her. In fact, Bandera had asked him if he wanted to take Mimi and Nanette up in one of their hot air balloons at their honeymoon resort. Be a real family, Bandera had said, but Mason had waved him off, as he waved off all his brothers about everything.

"Damnation," Mason said under his breath, wondering just how much his brothers had figured out. And if he found out that they did know—or that Mimi had told any of them—he was going to put a firm boot up any brother's ass that hadn't shared the news. If he found out that any brother of his had sided with Mimi by keeping such a secret from him…

His neck felt tight, and his skin turned hot. Mason told himself to calm down. He wouldn't be so angry if Mimi had told him in the first place, and for that he would never forgive her. Anger brewed deep inside him. How could she?

Because life was a game with Mimi Cannady. She was fun and high-spirited, and he'd always loved that side of her the best. Funny how he hadn't expected the very side that lured him to be his downfall.

His chest became even tighter as he wondered who else had known he was a father. Brian, of course. Widow Fancy knew because he'd made her look up the birth certificate Mimi had filed in the county records. There, plain as could be, was *Mason Jefferson* typed on the line for *Father.* No doubt the sheriff knew, as well.

Embarrassment burned inside him.

"Bro."

"Shh." Mason turned to look at Last, who had poked his head around the door. "What are you doing here?"

"Valentine and I left a cake on the table for Helga. Tomorrow is her birthday. We want you to hide— What's wrong?"

Mason shook his head. "Nothing."

"Something's wrong. You look like you've got a stomachache."

"No."

Last frowned at him. "Okay. I still say you look like you ate something that didn't agree, and you're always pretty sour looking, Mason, so if I think—"

"Last, get the hell out," Mason said, his voice low.

Last disappeared from the doorway. Nanette turned over in her sleep, her eyes closed tightly like a china doll's. Surely she was the most beautiful thing he'd ever laid eyes on, Mason decided. She'd always been a lovely little sprite moving through his life; he'd always loved her. But now that she was all his, love for her nestled even deeper inside his heart.

He was very angry with Mimi for stealing his time with Nanette from him, but she'd given him a wonderful miracle, too, he slowly admitted. Who could have imagined that something as sweet as a child could come from such a moment of fiery lovemaking?

After that night with Mimi, he'd felt guilt. He'd felt remorse, and he'd felt crazed in the head. But he'd never regretted it. It would be a lie to say he had. Even when she'd walked down the aisle with Brian, Mason had been glad he'd loved her. All practicality told him that she was better off with Brian, and he'd let her go. It had never been his intention to steal her away from her intended.

Only he supposed he had. Mimi couldn't have conceived a child with Brian while she was pregnant with Mason's child, and he supposed Brian hadn't wanted to raise another man's baby. It would have been too much for a new marriage to handle. He felt momentary guilt that perhaps she'd never had a chance to make her marriage work because of him.

The fact was, he couldn't keep his thoughts away from her, and that night he couldn't keep his hands off her. She'd been upset over her father's condition, and he'd comforted her. Without planning it, he had allowed that comfort to spiral into acting on his feelings and he had made love to her with every fiber of his being.

No, he didn't regret that. And her marriage… well, that was one more seed of guilt he'd end up reaping one day.

He sat up, astonishment hitting him. *"Nanette Jefferson,"* he said out loud. Not Cannady. Jefferson!

"Mason," Last said, peering around the door more cautiously this time, "I hate like hell to bother you, but—"

"That's my child," Mason said, pointing to Nanette gleefully.

"Yes, yes, she's our child, all of us adore her. But, Mason—"

Mason got up, barely able to keep the grin off his face. "That's my daughter. Not Brian's. *Mine.*"

Last stared at him. "Are you insane? Mason, I really think you need to come downstairs and let Calhoun and Fannin and me spell you for a bit. You've been working too hard."

"Nanette Jefferson," Mason said, stubborn in his joy.

"Are you…getting married?" Last asked.

"Hell, no," Mason said. "I'm getting proper papers filed, is what I'm going to do."

"Proper papers?" Last frowned. "To do what?"

"To declare Nanette as mine. To change her name. All that stuff that fathers do when they become fathers."

"Did you fall down the stairs and hit your head?"

"No," Mason said, "and when you figure it out, you'll realize you're Uncle Last."

Last blinked. "You're going to scare Mimi with all this crazy talk."

"Mimi scared me," Mason said. "She told me yesterday that Nanette is my child."

Last's jaw dropped. "So that's what Bandera was hinting about!"

"Bandera?" Mason stared at his youngest brother. "Does he know? Has he known all this time? And kept it from me?"

"Uh, I don't think so," Last said, clearly back-tracking or confused. "Now that I think of it, he said that he wished Nanette was your child so he could be Uncle Bandera."

"I'm going to put my boot—"

"I know, I know." Last held up his hand. "What difference does it make if Bandera knew, Mason? If Mimi had taken him into her confidence, he wouldn't tell you. None of us would go back on a confidence."

"She's my daughter!" Mason exclaimed. "I had a right to know!"

Last pulled him into the hall, closing the door. "Would you stop shouting into her subconscious?"

Mason blinked. "What?"

Last looked at him impatiently. "Nanette is hearing every word you say!"

"She's asleep."

"And hearing you bellyache. Now look, you can't be sore at all of us because once again you're all twisted up at Mimi. Mimi's had enough to deal with, and if she didn't figure you'd be much of a support system, then she didn't lean on you. She probably didn't tell you after she found out she was pregnant because she was married. For heaven's sake, Mason, you can understand that. After all, it's not exactly like Valentine was thrown a welcome reception by any of us when she told us she was pregnant with my daughter."

"Yeah, but you were having a weird phase."

"And you've been having a weird phase for years. I'm sure Mimi was scared out of her wits that you'd react somewhat the way you're reacting now."

"Mimi kept her from me," Mason said, angry.

"It's okay, Mason. It's not like Mimi had her in a different city and you never got to see her."

Mason glared at him. "She should have been on the ranch, where she belonged."

"And she was, most of the time. Mason, you should be happy you've got flesh and blood of your own without a wedding ring. You never wanted to get married, anyway." Last looked at him curiously. "So quit yer bitchin'."

Mason felt his chest heave. Last didn't understand. Mason didn't understand, himself. Too many new and different emotions were roiling his good sense.

"Jeez, Mason, I didn't spend any time with my daughter when she was young because I was being a jerk. You at least got to spend all the time you wanted with Nanette, and still can. Don't waste time being a dunce. That's all I have to say."

"It's not that easy."

The front door slammed. Both men peered over the stairwell in time to see a tiny blond whirlwind rush up the stairs. "I'm coming to kiss my daughter good-night, Mason," she said, brushing past the both of them, "so shut the hell up before you even say a thing."

"Whoa," Last said, "female troubles?"

"I don't know," Mason said, frowning. "I'd be the last person she'd share that with."

"Not her, Mason. You. Are *you* having female issues?" Last sighed with exasperation. "Are you and Mimi fighting?"

"Yes," Mason said. "I can answer that question affirmatively."

Last peered in the bedroom. Mason did, too, not really all that surprised that Mimi had decided to run right over his line in the sand. "Did you take Nanette from her, Mason?"

"Nanette belongs here, on the ranch that is her birthright," Mason said. "With her father."

"You ass," Last said under his breath. "You have no concept of how to woo a woman."

"I don't want to woo Mimi. I want to kick Mimi's little tail."

"Sure." Last nodded. "And you were saying that the whole time she was going down the aisle with

Brian—after you'd made love to her? I seem to remember sitting near you, and you looked pretty stone-faced, very determined to be Your Royal Hardheadedness."

Mimi stood, after making sure a sheet was tucked around Nanette. She placed Nanette's favorite small pink giraffe next to her, then Mimi walked to Mason and Last. "You're going to have to find a better way to handle this," she said. "You can't have everything your way. I know you're angry, but you're going to have to eventually calm down and think through what's best for Nanette."

She left, her sandals moving smartly down the stairs and out the door, which she closed quietly.

"She has a point, you know," Last said. "This could get weary for everyone if you don't chill out a bit." Last clapped him on the back. "Whoever would have thought you had it in you, you ol' sourpuss? After all the years you sang the Condom Song for us, specifically for *me*, it turns out you had a shower without your raincoat." Last grinned hugely, not about to be denied his crowing.

Mason sighed, knowing he full well had it coming—from all his brothers. "One time," he muttered. "One time."

"One shot's all it takes, bro," Last said gleefully.

"If your rifle's straight and well-oiled. And it appears you'd been taking good care of your equipment."

"Last," Mason said, his tone warning.

"Well," Last said, "I never thought I'd say this, but congratulations, Mason. You're a dad."

Mason was about to grunt a reply when Last continued. "A bachelor dad, of course. A single father. An unwedded man who will one day pay for prom gowns and wedding dresses."

Mason jutted out his chin. "Thank you, Last. You can go now."

Last turned serious. "Mason, it couldn't have happened to a nicer guy. Just be good to Mimi, okay? It's your future lying in there next to the little pink giraffe. You don't want to goof up the thing that means the most to you."

Last thundered down the stairs and went out the front door. Mason sighed, taking one last lingering look at his daughter, then headed toward his own room.

Last was right about one thing: Nanette was his future. And she was staying right here with him, where she belonged.

He would be generous and allow Mimi to visit whenever she wanted, though. Underneath his anger, he really didn't intend to keep her away from her child.

As long as everything went his way.

Chapter Three

Mimi knew one thing: Mason could not have his way, at least not the way he was trying to have it. She opened the door to his house early the next morning and set her own suitcase down. "Good morning, Helga," she said to the housekeeper, who was cleaning up after a very early breakfast. Two plates. One for Mason, one for Nanette. "Tomorrow, you can make breakfast for three."

Helga laughed. "Good. I wondered how long you'd stay away."

"Where are they?"

"In the fields. Nanette is going to learn how to ride fence this morning."

Mimi picked up her suitcase. "I'm going to hide this upstairs for now. At least until I spring some changes on Mason."

"Mr. Mason doesn't handle change very well," Helga said with a smile.

"He'd better learn to adapt. He's about to meet the even more stubborn side of Nanette's family tree." She went upstairs, trying to decide on the best place to sleep. There were several empty bedrooms that had been occupied by the Jefferson brothers over the years, and Nanette had been sleeping in the guest room.

Mason slept up here, too. A slight chill traveled over her skin as she gently swung open his bedroom door. His bed was made, and his dresser was tidy. A pair of jeans lay on the bed, as if he'd changed his mind about what he wanted to wear today. On the dresser was a picture of Mason and Nanette, posing beside Olivia's horse, Gypsy.

She knew she should be grateful that Mason was so crazy about their child.

"You can sleep in here," Helga said, her grin broad. "We can move Nanette here, too, and put Mason down the hall."

"I don't think so." Mimi backed away from Mason's room.

"A mother needs to be with her daughter," Helga commented. "Always I had Kelly with me."

Helga's daughter, Kelly, had married Fannin, one

of Mason's younger brothers. Mimi needed no reminder of how important the mother and child bond was. But moving into Mason's room was bound to start a fire of some kind. "Maybe we could push a small bed into the guest room Nanette is using."

"Hmm." The German housekeeper nodded. "We could. Mason is planning to decorate for Nanette. You might not like to stay in a room that is decorated with angels and bows."

Mimi smiled. "I really don't care about that." She crooked an eyebrow. "Angels and bows? Did Mason pick the decor?"

"Yes. In a catalog from England." Helga took a catalog from Mason's side table. "This is Daddy's idea of what his little girl should have."

Mimi was stunned. "It's breathtaking. And it costs a fortune!"

Helga grinned. "She's his only child."

Mimi blinked. "But such extravagance! That's not like Mason at all!"

"It's good for him. Let him spend. He is celebrating."

"I guess so," Mimi murmured. He was crazy. "I don't suppose he ordered the matching pink three-story dollhouse, as well?"

What sounded suspiciously like a giggle escaped

the stoutly built woman. "Of course. Nothing less than heaven for his little girl."

Mimi's heart curled tightly inside her. A very sad part of her was saying that they'd messed this whole thing up very badly. She and Mason would have been a good team: friends, lovers, excellent parents. Why had he not loved her enough to ask her to marry him?

Now it was really too late. She knew that by the way he was making plans without her. What father selected his little girl's room decor on his own? "What did he say when he told you?" Mimi asked, her heart so tight she could barely stand it.

"He told me that Nanette was his child. Which I had already known." Helga shrugged.

"You couldn't have," Mimi said. "I didn't tell anyone except Bandera, whom I swore to secrecy."

"Pfft. You and Brian were never together long enough to make anything happen."

"Neither were Mason and I, really," Mimi said.

"But it happened. And she looks just like him, anyway." Helga folded her arms with satisfaction. "I was making dinner when he called all his brothers, and I can tell you that he was quite proud. He bragged, actually, about his little daughter."

"He can be so odd," Mimi said with a reluctant smile. "I want to be so angry with him for taking

Nanette out of my house like a caveman, but part of me admires the side of him fatherhood has brought out."

"Very possessive. Good in a man," Helga said with a nod.

Mimi wrinkled her nose. "I don't know." She sighed. "We grew up playing with goats...and rope swings...and playing pranks on people for fun. We were a renegade band, me and the Jefferson boys. I would have been so lonely without the Jefferson kids. She'll be lonely out here." Mimi sighed. "At least in town there are many children for Nanette to play with."

Helga laughed. "Have another baby."

Mimi stared at her. "I don't really know what to say to that. How? Why? With whom?"

The housekeeper smiled. "Same way as the first time. Why? So Nanette won't be lonely. Although I think another baby would be more for you. And the only man you want to father your children is Mason. So, with Mason. That would be best for everyone."

Mimi jumped as she heard Mason's boots coming up the stairs. "Uh-oh."

Helga drifted away, leaving Mimi to face Mason alone.

"What are you doing?" Mason said when he saw Mimi. He noted her suitcase and frowned.

"Well, if you won't come to the mountain, the

mountain must go to you. Or something like that," she said, feeling very, very nervous.

"Meaning?" he asked with a bigger frown.

"That I'm moving in." She lifted her chin defiantly, waiting for the storm to erupt.

He shrugged. "Make yourself at home. Pick a room, and ask Helga for towels. Excuse me."

He disappeared into his bedroom and closed the door. She stood in the hall, her mouth open. Helga peeked her head from around a door frame and gave her a grin before disappearing again.

Mason's bedroom door jerked open, scaring her half out of her wits, since she hadn't fully recovered from his acceptance of her decision. She was still in fight-or-flight mode, and the adrenaline hadn't had time to filter through her body.

"Nanette's downstairs eating her peanut butter and jelly sandwich. Can you go watch her for me? I need a shower."

He closed the door. Mimi stood still for one second, then hurried down the stairs. Nanette sat at the table, chewing happily, her hair prickly with straw pieces. "Sweetie!" Mimi exclaimed. "I've missed you!" She hugged and kissed her daughter with delight.

Nanette handed her a piece of sandwich. Mimi shook her head. "No, thank you. But it looks delicious."

"Uncle Mason made it," Nanette said.

"Oh." Obviously, Mason hadn't seen fit to enlighten his daughter to what he was apparently crowing all over the town and to all his brothers. Mimi wondered why Mason hadn't told Nanette the truth.

Maybe it was because she was so very young. Mimi sat next to her daughter on the bench, wondering how Nanette would react to a truth that would change her life. Was changing it even now.

All thanks to Mason. He was in the process of changing Nanette's world to the way he thought it should be—and didn't seem too inclined to include Mimi in his plans.

MASON STOOD UNDER a hot shower, letting the water run over his muscles. He was tense, more from the fact that Mimi was in his house and likely to cause more trouble than from any labor he'd performed.

She had changed his world. With her typical dive into unthinking actions, she had sent him on new paths he'd never thought of exploring. He was a father, had been a father, and she had stolen his chances to experience the wonder of fatherhood fully. She would have justification and reasoning, but this time he would not allow her to sway his mind.

He was extremely angry with her. He wasn't certain he could forgive her.

And yet, for Nanette's sake, he was going to have to learn to live with the fact that Mimi was now an inescapable part of his life. There was no running from her or ignoring her now. Over the years, he'd mainly shoved his feelings about Mimi to the background.

Now, in spite of his anger, a very secret part of him was relieved that they were inextricably tied together—and forever so. Another part of him was deeply grateful that she'd given him a child. It was mind-bending, and he hadn't expected the overwhelming rush of proprietary emotions that came with fatherhood.

So, good or bad, Mimi was impacting him, as always, only on a new level. He should expect Mimi's influence in his life to grow ever more profound. Good or bad, then: what to do about Mimi?

For Nanette's sake, he should marry Mimi. Mason stood under the water, unblinking, as the foreign thought stayed in his mind, echoing. For Nanette's sake....

He shut off the water and toweled off slowly. What other option was there? Providing his daughter with a whole home and family would be the right thing to do.

He had done the right thing all his life. When Maverick left, Mason and his brothers should have been put into foster care. But Union Junction was a small town, and people had known Maverick and his beloved wife. The boys were in church every Sunday and in school during the week. Townspeople weren't anxious to see a grieved family split up, so Sheriff Cannady stepped in, saying he'd keep an eye on the Jefferson boys. Papers that should have been filed somehow never were; reports to authorities were never made. The family stayed together.

Everyone figured Maverick would come back. By the time anybody finally realized the boys were completely on their own, Mason had turned eighteen, legal age to raise a family if need be. He had done right by his brothers, and Mason was damn proud of it. Family was what made daily existence meaningful. Otherwise life would be simply survival in a lonely, empty void.

Mimi was now part of his family, in a way that no game of pretend between playmates could have made it so. He needed to do right by her and Nanette. But if he was going to marry Mimi, there was a price to pay, and he damn sure expected to make her pay it.

A man needed to be the head of his household. No Mimi-hijinks, or his world would stay continually unsettled. If she thought that because she'd moved herself in here—a fact he admired—she could run his household and therefore his life, she was in for a rude awakening.

If she thought that now that the truth had come out, he would pursue her, she would find herself wrong about that, as well. His brothers had pursued their women, gaga and smitten, until they caught their prey. But he was no hunter. His driving need was for a family that contained no fracture, and he would not play the games of courtship.

Mimi would need to accept his terms.

But first, he intended to let her stew in her own worry and uncertainty, just as he'd done ever since she'd dropped her emotional bomb on him. In fact, she'd dropped a lot of emotional bombs on him over the years, and he was in no hurry to put away his bomb shelter.

Dressed now, he went downstairs to check on Nanette. His daughter sat contentedly working a puzzle, and her mother sat next to her. Mimi looked up at him. "We need to talk."

He nodded. "I know."

She hesitated. "Do you have your schedule at hand so I can pencil in an appointment?"

"I have time now." Might as well see what was on her mind.

"Well, I think it needs to be in private," Mimi said, her tone uncertain.

"Helga!" Mason called up the stairwell. "Could you come watch Nanette for a few minutes?"

The housekeeper came down the stairs with a smile. "Yes. In fact, I am going into town to check on the sheriff—oh. Sorry," she said to Mason. "You are sheriff now."

He shook his head. "Sheriff Cannady will always be 'Sheriff' to me, as well."

Helga smiled. "I have some chicken soup to put on for him."

Relief was on Mimi's face, and Mason knew that she hadn't quite worked out the details of how she was going to stay here with him and Nanette, and yet spend time with her father. Helga had long been taking care of both households. Clearly, Mimi was grateful that could continue, as it would be a bit difficult for her to cook here and then run food into town to the sheriff. Plus, she'd just get under Helga's feet, though Helga was likely too wonderful to complain about Mimi intruding in her kitchen.

"Thank you," Mimi said.

"I will take him his granddaughter—if I may," Helga said to Mason.

Mason nodded. "She'd love to see her grandfather. Thank you."

Helga gathered up some things as Mason stared at Mimi. Clearly nervous, she plucked at a table napkin. They needed time alone, he decided. This would give him a chance to tell Mimi what he expected from this new partnership between the two of them. He was pretty certain he was calm enough now to discuss what she'd done.

Then again, maybe he'd just roar all over her for keeping his daughter from him. Mason took a deep breath, and kissed his daughter. "I'll see you for dinner, Nanette. Mind Ms. Helga."

"I will." She slid off the bench, gave her mother a hug and skipped out the door with Helga. The front door closed firmly.

"Mason—" Mimi began.

Instantly, he held up a hand. From the first word, he intended to let her know that this was his house, that was his daughter and he was in charge. "Mimi."

She fell silent. For a moment, he admired her face. Though they were both older now, she retained a sweet expression—when she wasn't being mulish—and a girl's curves. Her jeans were filled out in the right places, and her white blouse was untucked and plain, again showing pleasing curves.

He did remember he'd enjoyed the act of creating Nanette, even if he hadn't known they were doing so at the time.

"Mimi," he said more sternly to get his mind off his wandering thoughts. "I will probably never forgive you for keeping my daughter from me."

Her shoulders stiffened. "I don't expect you to. I'm not asking you to."

He felt his teeth go slightly on edge at her unyielding reply. "All right. What topic did you think was important enough to call a caucus?"

She looked around. "Caucus? It's just you and me. That's a conversation, one between two people who now have similar goals. Mine is to see Nanette happy as she grows into a responsible young lady, and yours is to see Nanette happy as she grows into a responsible young lady."

His mouth twisted. "The conversation topic, then, please. I have a lot to do today."

"I want to be present when you tell Nanette that you're her father. I think we should do it as a family."

He blinked, caught by surprise. He'd expected her to argue about Nanette living with him. Actually, he had deliberately left his mind open to any shock she might throw his way, because it was Mimi he was dealing with. But this one was bigger than he'd expected.

He narrowed his gaze. "I would think that would be the obvious way to go about it."

"You always thought everything was obvious. Most of us couldn't measure up to your vision of plain-in-sight."

Now he was getting steamed, and he really had meant to stay calm, rational and focused in all his dealings with the mother of his child. *Respect,* he told himself. *Respect the mother of your child, even when she has that tone that only Mimi knows how to deliver so effectively.*

"Us?"

"Never mind." She waved a hand. "Let's just focus on the future."

"Fine by me." He crossed his arms, glaring.

"Would you grant me that, Mason? I need to be present when you tell Nanette that you're not her uncle. She's going to be so surprised, and she's going to have a lot of questions. I think I'm the appropriate person to give her the level of information she will need."

He didn't want to upset his child, that was for certain. And if Mimi could help smooth his transition from uncle to father… "We should probably talk as a family," he conceded.

"Thank you." Mimi flashed him a smile women

usually gave men in black-and-white Westerns, as if he was a hero or something.

Mason knew he was no hero. She was working him like a steer. "Mimi, no drama."

"What are you talking about?" The grateful smile slid off her face.

"I want to keep it very simple between you and me. While I appreciate the fact that you've moved into my house, we need to establish some basic rules. We make appointments to chat with each other about Nanette. You cause no disruptions. You make no decisions for me or my household. In return, you can stay here rent-free."

Mimi gasped. "You jerk! You arrogant, pigheaded son of a—"

He held up a lordly hand. "Mimi, no drama, no disruptions."

Mimi's lips pursed. "You are an ass, as always. I will never know why I loved you all those years."

Her hand flew over her mouth, but Mason couldn't say who was more shocked, Mimi or him. They stared at each other, dumbfounded. He couldn't process her confession fast enough, her statement too large to take in, and before he understood what she was doing, Mimi had grabbed her purse and run out the front door.

His jaw could hardly be more loose if it was a separate, oiled and hinged piece of his face. "Loved me?" he repeated to himself, stunned. "Loved me all those *years?*"

Chapter Four

What in the hell was Mimi talking about? Mason told himself not to listen, not to get sucked into Mimi-schemies, but his bomb shelter wasn't completely protected against such an onslaught. He stalked out after her, catching her before she could back her truck down the driveway. Without thinking, he jerked her door open. "Stop," he demanded.

"No, Mason."

He reached in, switched off the engine, pulled her out and kicked the door shut with a boot, gently dragging a reluctant Mimi into the house. "Explain."

"No!"

He sat her on the sofa and walked a safe space across the room. "I think you'd best speak now or forever hold your peace."

Mimi was silent. Then she sighed. "Mason, it's no

secret to anyone in this town, or to your brothers, or just about anyone else. I did love you. I guess all my life."

"We were friends! You couldn't have loved me."

Mimi shrugged, wiping away something on her face. Mason told himself stubbornly that it was a piece of grass, or dirt—anything other than tears.

"You might not have loved me, but I loved you." Mimi looked away from him. "I've made jokes about being the girl who could never get her man. So if your feelings are hurt because I didn't tell you that Nanette was your child, think of how I felt loving you and finding myself pregnant with a child I knew you…wouldn't want."

"I would have wanted her," Mason said, feeling himself get angry again.

"You want her because you know her now," Mimi said, "but if I'd come to you and told you I was pregnant, you would have thought I was trying to trap you into marriage. You're always suspecting me of a scheme."

He froze, right in the middle of thinking that very thought.

"Would you have been able to conceive of what having a child would mean to you, Mason? *Now* you know Nanette, and the two of you are inseparable. But I don't think you would have welcomed the news of a pregnancy then. You were dealing with Last, and your father, and I was married…it was far better to continue on the course I was on. At least I thought so at the time. You know, sometimes life is messy, Mason, but it's not always because I want it to be that way." She took a deep breath. "Actually, all my life I've wanted stability. I think any child who grows up without a mother wants that, and since you and I both lost ours, you should understand more than anyone how much I want a stable home life for Nanette."

"I'm sorry," Mason said, surprising himself. "So you *did* love me?"

"Mason," Mimi said impatiently. "Don't make me repeat it."

He shook his head. "But you said it past tense."

She looked at him. "Past tense?"

"You said you'd *loved* me."

"Oh." Mimi blushed a becoming pink that went nicely with her blond hair and delicate features. "Well, it was a long time ago."

"I see," Mason said, somewhat deflated. Gathering his pride, he nodded. "Thank you for your honesty. It makes having to live under the same roof easier."

Mimi turned to go. Mason felt as if he needed to

say something to make her stay. "For what's it's worth, I never stopped thinking about that night."

She slowly turned to look at him.

"And I mean, I guess I could say that I knew she was my daughter, that there was this instant connection. But I thought that connection was because I helped you deliver her. Nanette was just this writhing, wailing bundle of baby, and I never doubted she was Brian's. So you're right. I wasn't ready to be a father. I'm sure I wasn't. I'd been avoiding it too long, because I'd already raised eleven brothers."

"So try to forgive me," Mimi said. "I'm certainly going to try to forgive you."

He straightened, all his good intentions flying away. "Forgive *me?* For what?"

"All the times you were a donkey's butt. When you never noticed me. When you didn't notice that I was desperately in love with you. I forgive you for not noticing that I wanted to be more than a friend to you, more than a sister. And I forgive you for not psychically knowing that Nanette was yours so I wouldn't have to make such a difficult confession."

"So okay, I forgive you for not psychically knowing that you should have told me sooner! Mimi Cannady, you waited too long to tell me!" he thundered. Then he took a deep breath. "Let's just stick to the basics. We tell Nanette together and otherwise peaceably coexist."

"Thank you," Mimi said, in that snippy tone he knew too well, "that was all *I* wanted." She turned to leave again, opening the door, but by now, his emotions had the best of him.

"Well, it's not all I want," he said, closing the door and picking her up. He carried her up the stairs, ignoring her wriggling. "First, I'm going to give you what you deserve."

"You're going to do no such thing!"

Mimi bit his arm lightly, but he ignored that, too. He'd been through a lot of pain in his life, and a little nip didn't bother him. "I believe I overheard you tell Helga you were worried that Nanette would be lonely out here on the ranch, so let's just see what we can do about that, shall we?"

He laid her gently on his bed. "You're beautiful," he said. "Stubborn, but beautiful."

She tried to sit up. He sat next to her, kissing her the way he'd wanted to the night they were together. "I never forgot that night," he said, his throat husky. "I always wanted to be with you again."

His words melted her resistance. She lay back down, pulling him with her. "Come on, cowboy. Keep talking sweet. I've waited years to hear you romance me." She pulled off his shirt and unzipped his jeans.

"It's only fair to tell you that I don't have marriage on my mind," he said, yanking off her shirt and pulling her jeans down.

She laughed. "I don't recall proposing to you."

He hesitated. "I'm supposed to do the proposing."

Her smile was seductive. "Mason, you worry too much about being the boss. If you want to be a man, take my panties off."

"Mason!" he heard bellowed up the stairwell. "Mason, are you home?"

He got into bed next to Mimi and pulled the covers up over both of them. "It's Calhoun," he said. "Don't say a word. Probably wants me to help fix his windmill. Or corral Gypsy. Or watch the kids. If we lie here, he'll go away."

Mimi giggled. The door echoed with pounding, and then it swung open.

"Ya napping, Mason?" Calhoun asked, peering around the door. "I need...oh." His gaze widened at the sight of Mimi and Mason propped against the pillows, sheets up to their armpits. "I *beg* your pardon."

"It's worse than it looks," Mason said with a sigh.

"Actually, it looks good to me," Calhoun said. "I'll be going now."

"Is it an emergency?" Mason asked.

"No. Kenny and Minnie want to play with Nanette, so I was going to help you fix the dock so they could swim. But it can wait. Bye, Mimi. Good to see you finally caught the old cuss." Calhoun slammed the door.

Mason rolled his eyes, preparing to strip his jeans and make sweet afternoon delight with Mimi, but she jumped from the bed and began dressing as fast as she could.

"Hey!" he exclaimed. "Get back in my bed!"

"No," Mimi said, going to the door so he couldn't haul her back in. "Do you know, I forgot about Minnie and Kenny?"

"What the hell do they have to do with this?" Mason asked, pointing to the bed.

"Nanette won't be lonely. We don't need to have more children. In fact, we *shouldn't* have more children. We don't even know if we work together. As we are, that is," Mimi said. "It could be awkward, you know. Both of us under the same roof. Parenting together. Et cetera."

"It's already awkward," Mason grumbled, feeling as if the tent in his jeans was pressing the breath out of him. "Mimi, let's continue our discussion."

"Not a good idea, and we've been frugal with

good ideas our whole friendship," Mimi said, hurrying out the door. "We should be frugal with the bad ones, as well. Bye, Mason!"

Mason could hear her feet tripping lightly down the stairs. Sighing, he knew full well he'd missed a prime opportunity to get on top in their relationship.

And it wasn't just sex he was worried about.

He picked up her bra off the floor and smiled. Oh, he would get on top—and it would be sooner rather than later, he vowed. Mimi Cannady was going to learn that he was a man to be reckoned with, and if she thought he was going to chase her, she was quite mistaken. Mimi was going to do all the chasing, until she understood that not only had she loved him, she still did.

He was the only man she would ever love, no matter how much she wanted to believe otherwise.

Then it hit him: Mimi had turned the tables on him. She had tricked him into wanting her. Despite his best promises to himself, he had fallen into her charming net, happily and gladly.

Now that he'd kissed her again, and tasted her, it might even be an irrevocable fall—which was exactly what he'd been avoiding for years.

He didn't want to fall mindlessly as his brothers had. He'd seen what that had done to their lives.

While the end results might be happy and beneficial for them, getting there looked messy and torturous.

He'd had enough of that.

She's right. No more bad ideas. No more Mimi, he told himself for the thousandth time.

The problem was, as wonderful as it had been to make love to the girl she'd been, the woman she was now would be far more satisfying. His soul ached to its very core that he must deny himself that sweetness. But he had to, or he would be lost—like Maverick, the father who had eventually succumbed to his broken heart.

Chapter Five

Word of the afternoon she hadn't really spent with Mason somehow got around like cookies at a bridal shower. Mimi couldn't understand how so many people seemed to think that she and Mason were now destined for the altar. The knowing winks and happy smiles and the well-meaning question *Where is Sheriff Jefferson this afternoon?* were all somewhat embarrassing.

Darn Calhoun and his big Jefferson mouth.

"He means well," the stylists at the Union Junction Salon agreed once they heard her story. All the girls were there, including Valentine, who had closed up at the bakery. Everyone gathered to sit out on the lawn, enjoy some lemonade and a gossip among girls. Sighing, Mimi recognized how much these special times among her "sisters" meant to her.

"Calhoun might have meant well, but what he thought happened, didn't. The truth is that Mason and I are farther apart than ever. I don't even know why I say 'Mason and I' in the same breath. Separate is what we have to be."

The women looked at her. There were nineteen stylists who'd come to Union Junction several years ago and stayed through the night of the big storm that had nearly leveled the town. They'd worked for a while in Lonely Hearts Station before Last's girlfriend, Valentine, accidentally burned down the salon. Now they were all back here. The only missing "sister" was Annabelle Turnberry Jefferson, who lived in a different city with her husband, Frisco Joe. Over the years, all the women had grown close, a family who had learned to be strong despite whatever bad circumstance had originally brought them here.

Mimi felt certain she shouldn't complain about her life, when it was as wonderful as it was, but one too many people had asked about Mason. Mimi had replied that she wasn't in charge of his social calendar, which had gotten the girls to gossiping.

"You can't give up on him," Marni said. "He's the father of your child."

"You know how those Jeffersons are," Lily said. "Irresistible. Though I love my Sam."

Mimi shook her head. "I've known the Jeffersons all my life. They are not irresistible."

"You told us they were," Valentine said with a laugh. "Remember?"

"I didn't want to burst your bubbles. Yours or Olivia's or anybody else's who chose to marry one."

"You love Mason," Daisy said. She grinned. "And you protest too much."

"Loving someone doesn't mean you're right for each other," Mimi said primly. "Mason and I aren't a good match."

The ladies smiled.

"You want him to chase you," someone suggested. "You want to know that he wants you and not just because you had a child with him."

Mimi thought about that for a minute. Her pride pricked her far too much to allow herself to admit that perhaps she felt just that way. "We just wouldn't work. We've been friends too long."

"Then how'd you end up in bed together naked?" Shasta asked. "Which, by the way, sounds like a great way to spend an afternoon."

Mimi blushed. "Momentary insanity."

"And the fact that he's gorgeous doesn't hurt," someone said.

"Nor does it hurt that he's the sheriff. Mason looks great in a hat and badge."

"But he looked great in nothing but his hat, huh, Mimi?"

Everyone laughed except Mimi. She stared at the ladies, stricken, and then sighed.

"We're not trying to hurt your feelings," Shasta said, going over to hug her. "We're just trying to help you sort it out. It sure sounds like you like him, and we think you still love him, and we want to help."

"You can't," Mimi said. "He's an ape."

"But a hot ape," Dixie said. "All men are stubborn in some way."

"Yes," Mimi said, "but the moment was gone for me after my divorce was final, and before he found out about Nanette. I knew that if he loved me, he would speed to my side in hot pursuit. After all, I was free. And I'd been waiting for him forever. But no," Mimi said, shaking her head, "it was the same as it's always been. Just friends."

"Ew," Gretchen said, "the kiss of death for relationships."

"Thank you," Tisha replied. "That helped a lot."

"She's right," Mimi said. "I knew it was time to face that fact myself."

The phone rang, and Violet picked it up. Mimi

barely listened as her name was called. "It's Julia Finehurst, Mimi."

Julia was her best friend, and Julia's Honey-Do Agency was very successful. She crowed pretty often about sorting out the troubles at Malfunction Junction. Julia and her agency had accidentally sent the stylists to town several years ago, in response to Mimi's request for a housekeeper for Mason. It wasn't until Julia's second try at solving the house-keeping problem that Mason hired Helga. Unfortu-nately, there were some troubles that not even a best friend could sort out.

"I haven't been able to get you in days," Julia complained. "Your dad says you're staying at Mal-function Junction for a while. Are you trying to catch the last bachelor out there?"

Mimi winced. "Not exactly."

"Oh. I thought maybe if you were staying out there, that you and Mason—"

"No. Mason has other plans, and they don't really include me."

"Mason's always included you in all his plans," Julia said reasonably. "You're usually the one making his plans for him."

"They're not all so easy to make," Mimi said, aware that the ladies were listening, though they tried to appear as if they weren't. "I told him that he was Nanette's father, and he moved Nanette to the ranch. I had no choice but to follow."

"Oh. So, being one big happy family is difficult?" Julia asked.

"I'll say."

"Hmm. Mimi, he's a man. He can be caught."

Mimi blinked. "I don't know much about catching anything, really."

"Well," Julia said, "you're just going to have to make him love you. For Nanette's sake. It's the kindest thing for him, Mimi. Once he's dragged down the aisle, he'll appreciate it."

"I'll see you this weekend," Mimi said softly, knowing that none of what Julia was saying applied to Mason. He was much too contrary for any plan to work with him.

"You remember what I said," Julia said. "He's a man. Just set out the right bait, and you'll catch him. If you don't have the right bait, I can send you some."

"No, thank you," Mimi said. "I already tried bait and ended up married to someone else." She hung up, and looked at the ladies who were now staring at her openly. "Julia thinks I'm not using the right lure."

"But you said you didn't want to catch him," Beatrice said. "We think you want him to catch you."

"I want it not to be this hard," Mimi said crossly. "Love should be simple. The recipe is that I fall in love with a man, and he falls in love with me, and we live happily ever after."

"Someone read you Grimm's fairy-tale cookbook," Remy said. "No one I know has that kind of marriage."

"Well, they should," Mimi insisted. "I've waited all my life to be loved by the right man. I've had my father as a role model, and I know that waiting on the right love is the only way to go. Mason isn't that man. At least not for me."

She looked around at her friends from the Union Junction Salon and Lonely Hearts Salon—this group of women had been through a lot, and they'd adopted her as one of them from the beginning. She could tell them anything. "My father says Mason needs some space," Mimi confided.

"Space!" The ladies chuckled. "Honey, if you give a man too much space, he gets lost," Jessica said.

"Maybe he just needs some time to sort things out," Mimi said. "I did drop a very big piece of news into his world. He's adjusting to being a father." She took a breath. "I always loved Mason, and I always hoped he'd see me as someone he was in love with. Then we…were together—" She knew guilt flashed over her face. "We just lost our minds that night. I know it sounds cliché, but you know what? That's what I want to happen again," she said softly.

"Ohhhh," they all said.

"You want him wild for you," Daisy said.

"I want to know that we can both find our way back together after everything we've been through. And that the magic we felt that night is still there."

"Maybe Mason's suppressing it," Lily suggested. "Men suppress a lot of things."

Through the window they saw Crockett walk onto the lawn across the street and go straight to Valentine, giving her a big kiss on the lips. Everyone went *mmm,* though Valentine suddenly looked as if she was wearing blush.

That is what I want, Mimi thought. *I want Mason to want me that much, and not be afraid to show it.*

The chance of that happening at this point, she supposed, was next to nothing. Though they had nearly wound up making a dreadful mistake in his bedroom yesterday, the real problem was that Mason was not crazy about her.

It took crazy to make a marriage work.

"What are you doing here, Crockett?" someone called out the open door, "besides bussing Valentine?"

"Picking up my daughter," he replied. "She's been with Momma long enough," he said with a wink to

Valentine. "Besides, Mason wants her to come out to the ranch to play with Nanette."

Mimi's eyes went wide. Mason was making a play date for Nanette? He didn't think he needed to consult her?

Obviously, Mason thought he was in charge. Of the town, his brothers, his daughter. Mimi's head spun. She wanted him to ask her opinion about what made Nanette happy. Of course, he'd known Nanette for so long that he already knew what made her happy.

Mimi sighed. This living together was going to be tough. He wasn't going to be the kind of housemate who made lots of mutual decisions.

"So what are you girls doing?" Crockett asked with a lazy grin for the gathering. "Hen talking?"

"We're trying to figure out how to catch a cowboy," someone said brightly.

He shrugged with a devilish twinkle in his eyes. "All the good ones are taken."

"Except Mason," Kiki boldly said.

"Well, yes," Crockett said with a fast glance at Mimi, "though I believe his daughter has stolen his heart."

Mimi looked toward Kiki, astonished by her comment and wondering what the woman was up to.

"Say someone wanted to catch Mason," another girl said. "What would be the ideal way to his heart?"

"Oh, no," Crockett said, shaking his head. "You're not getting me into that trap. I know what you ladies are up to. Matchmaking. And if you think that getting Mason and Mimi together is just a simple matter of striking a match, you haven't realized the toughness of the tinder. Mason is not a fire easily lit."

"Come on, Crockett," Velvet said. "We're getting good at this wedding shower stuff. We'd like to throw one for Mimi, too."

"You're gonna have to give him a kick in the ass and a slap upside his stubbornly concrete head," Crockett said. "That's pretty much what worked with me."

"Okay," Mimi said, rising. "I need to have some dignity. It's not like I think Mason and I are the perfect match or anything. I thank everyone for their kind thoughts on my behalf. I've had advice as simple as slapping him, giving him space and catching him. However," she said with a smile, "when something is right, it is right. And I can't overlook the fact that while Mason and I may have some attraction to each other, and while we may be friends, we are not inclined to wedded bliss. It's just as much my issue as his."

"We didn't mean any harm, Mimi," Marni said.

"I know. You didn't! In fact, I really appreciate everyone being so concerned about my happiness."

She smiled at them. "I'm really blessed. If you think about it, my life is perfect. I have a wonderful father, a beautiful daughter, all of you, and Mason's friendship. This is just a new page in my book with Mason."

"Well, it's a thriller," Carly said. "We'll keep reading."

"I know," Mimi said with a laugh. "That's why I love you all so much."

All of them, every single one of them, had tried to help, and Mimi left feeling much better.

It was true—she did have everything. The past few years her life had been filled with many challenges, but she'd withstood them. She was strong enough to be a single mother and to accept that her teenage dreams of a starry honeymoon with Mason were nothing but fairy dust.

Twenty minutes later, she was back at the ranch. Nanette and Annette were playing in a sandbox that Mason and Crockett were busily filling with soft, white sand.

The fact is, Mimi told herself, *he is an awesome father, just like Maverick was. Nanette will never know a moment of uncertainty as long as Mason is around.*

Her heart filled with understanding, both of her own feelings and for Mason. It was going to be all right.

"Hi," Mason said as she walked toward them.

"Hi," she said with a smile for the brothers and the little girls. "What a beautiful sandbox."

Nanette took a bucketful and poured it over Annette's stubby legs. Mimi smiled at Mason. "This is a great idea."

"It was your father's," Mason said. "He said you'd always wanted one when you were growing up, and that he'd been busy sheriffing and raising a child alone, so he never got around to it. Kept telling himself he had plenty of time, and then, he said, one day you were all grown up. The time for sandboxes had passed."

Mimi stared at Mason. A lump grew inside her throat that felt strange and heavy with sentimental emotions. She wanted to say *thank you for caring about Nanette* or *I never knew my father felt that way,* but there was really no reason to speak. It was enough to know that something as simple as a sandbox mattered that much to Mason.

Chapter Six

Mason watched, astonished, as Mimi turned and went inside the house. "What just happened?" he asked Crockett.

"Girl stuff," Crockett said. "Not to oversimplify, but you hit her in the female zone. It's even better than giving her flowers. You got her all choked up and misty, and now she's not going to be mad at you anymore for luring her into bed like Calhoun told me you did."

Mason blinked. "I did not lure her. And why does everything in this family have to be a topic of discussion?"

"Because we're cool like that. We care about each other. And mainly, you shocked Calhoun so bad that he almost needed therapy. He would have been less surprised to see a dragon on the other side of that door. I mean, you and Mimi haven't exactly—"

"All right," Mason said crossly. "I get the picture."

"In fact," Crockett said, "since you've never had a woman to the ranch, or a girlfriend, we were beginning to think you were, you know—"

"No," Mason said, "I don't. Fill me in."

"Well, disinterested is the first word that comes to mind."

"Let it be the last word," Mason said. "Just because I didn't carry on elaborate plans to bed women doesn't mean I wasn't interested. I was setting an example for my younger brothers. That's why I went to the trouble of creating a jingle I called the Condom Song—I needed something simple for you boneheads to remember whenever you got your urges." Mason grunted. "Not that it did any good for most of you."

"Nor you, apparently," Crockett said. "But we love our little niece." He grinned at the kids in the sandbox. "Anyway, what I was getting at is that you just made Mimi real happy with the sandbox and the ooey-gooey story about her dad wanting her to have one. You shouldn't have any trouble getting her back into the s—"

"Crockett," Mason said, "life is not all about sex." He dumped the last of the sand into the box and looked at it with satisfaction. "Maybe we should have had one of these when we were young."

Crockett slapped him on the shoulder. "If we had, you would have been forever wheezing about sand in the washing machine, bro. I gotta go. I've got a Valentine to get home to."

"Yeah. Sure," Mason said, watching as his brother walked toward his truck after kissing the little girls goodbye. "Thanks for helping me put this thing together."

Crockett was gone and the girls weren't paying Mason any attention, too delighted with their new toy to look up. Mason sat down on the ground, enjoying their pleasure, with only Crockett's words to prick at him.

They pricked like cactus needles, forcing him to try to find the source. He knew the source was Mimi, but it was more than that. The anger had passed. So had the shock. A curious sense of what-if was left in its place.

He had made so many mistakes. Heeding Sheriff Cannady's words, Mason didn't want to look back with regrets.

She was the most beautiful woman he had ever known. She made his heart sing and his blood crazy, and she'd given him a child.

He was really afraid of himself. What was he supposed to do—fall for a woman and then hope he didn't end up heartbroken one day? Heartbreak was mean and nasty and tore families apart.

"Hey," he heard a voice say.

Glancing up into the warm sun of summer, he saw his friends Hawk and Jellyfish had sneaked up on him. They were so quiet, in fact, that the girls sat in their sandbox, still giggling and running sand over the edge of the sandbox, completely engrossed.

Hawk and Jellyfish had been investigating Mason's father's whereabouts and they wouldn't be here if they didn't have something to discuss. Something that would require a decision on his part, or that would change the fabric of their family. One shock at a time was all he could take.

"Howdy," he said, standing. "Good to see you, friends." He nodded toward Nanette. "That's my daughter. Her name is Nanette."

Hawk and Jellyfish glanced at the child, studying her as she completely ignored them.

"Mimi's daughter," Hawk said.

"And mine," Mason said.

The two men nodded.

"Congratulations, Dad," Jellyfish said. "It must be groovy to have family you didn't know about."

Mason stared at him suspiciously. "Would that be a lead-in?"

Hawk silently handed him a journal. Leather-bound and small, no bigger than six by eight inches, it had seen better days. The pages were yellow, the brown leather as worn as well-beaten cowhide. Mason didn't open it. He didn't want to. He raised an eyebrow and waited.

"It's your father's," Hawk said unnecessarily. "It was sent to us by Mannie, the woman of Inuit descent he stayed with for some years. She found it hidden in a box of old clothes."

Mason swallowed. The small book would reveal the private thoughts of a man Mason had never stopped missing. He felt somewhat naked and exposed suddenly, with Hawk and Jellyfish watching him, and he quickly drew an expressionless curtain over his face.

"Daddy?" Nanette said, startling Mason so bad that his legs began to tremble. He stared at her, and she looked back at him with Mimi's guileless blue eyes. A hard knot of emotion fused his throat until he could barely draw a breath.

She called me Daddy. She's not supposed to know, because Mimi and I haven't told her. But I'm not Uncle anymore.

I'm Daddy.

Pride dashed through him, and the past rolled away. He kneeled down to hug his daughter, barely remembering he was still holding the journal filled with his father's handwriting. Someday he would deal with that. But not now. Right now, he was a father. "Go on up to the house, boys. Helga will get you something good to snack on."

They didn't say anything, but he knew Hawk and Jellyfish were gone. Maybe they'd left before he'd even said anything; those two had their own communication style. But the little arms around his neck right now were the only kind of communication Mason wanted.

MIMI WAS STARTLED when Hawk and Jellyfish appeared in the kitchen. "Hi!" she exclaimed. "When did you get here?"

"Not more than five minutes ago," Hawk said.

"Is Mason coming in, too?" Mimi asked, while Helga put food on plates for the men.

Jellyfish grinned. "He's chilling with his little girl right now."

"Oh." Mimi looked at the men uncomfortably. "Mason told you that Nanette was his daughter?"

"Yes." Hawk looked at her curiously. "And Nanette called him Daddy."

Mimi's eyes widened; her earth felt strangely off its center. How would Nanette have known?

"Someone in your family has strong powers of perception," Hawk said. "She's young for that, but it's a good thing."

"What?" Mimi said, her mind racing madly as she wondered about her daughter's welfare. If Nanette knew Mason was her father, then one day she was going to ask the question *Why aren't you and Daddy married? Why did you never marry?* These were questions Mimi hadn't previously considered. They scared her. The whys were complicated. Even she didn't understand them.

If she were a better, more organized mother, perhaps this wouldn't be so messy. For Nanette's sake, she wished she could have made everything neater in their lives. "Ugh," she said. "I need my own powers of perception to figure all this out."

"No." Hawk smiled appreciatively at the plate Helga put in front of him. "You already have them."

Jellyfish nodded. "Nanette would likely get them from you. None of the Jefferson men are particularly perceptive."

Hawk held up his fork and pointed at Jellyfish. "Or they are, but they just conceal their powers until they are overtaken by some life-altering event."

"Such as meeting their life mate," Jellyfish said, his brow wrinkling.

Mason and the girls came into the kitchen. Helga hugged the girls and took them upstairs, while Mason fixed himself a plate and sat down across from Mimi.

"So what are you going to do with the journal?" Hawk asked.

"Journal?" Mimi said, looking at Mason.

Mason shrugged. "I don't know. For now, I put it in a safe place." He looked at his friends. "I suppose you read it? For info-gathering purposes?"

Hawk looked horrified. "It is not good to read someone's private words. I don't read your mail, do I?"

"Sorry," Mason said. "I didn't think about that."

"It all comes down to powers of perception," Hawk said.

Mason's eyebrows rose. "Powers of perception?"

"Yes. You're suppressing them. You seek answers, but you don't really want them. For anything in your life."

"Oh." Mason sent a guilty look toward Mimi. "Now look, you fellows must be hungry. You're off the case for now, so just enjoy Helga's dinner."

Jellyfish looked at Mimi. "I would marry you," he said kindly, "but I never settle in one place for long."

Mimi looked at the large hippie throwback with some concern. "Thank you. But I'm fine. Really. Nanette is fine."

"What's wrong with Nanette?" Mason demanded, his head rearing.

"Nothing," Mimi said hastily, realizing that this topic was likely to provoke Mason.

"She has strong powers of perception," Hawk said. "She needs you to understand."

"Understand?" Mason's brow furrowed. "Nanette is a little girl and she's going to be just fine as long as she lives under my roof where I can protect her."

Hawk and Jellyfish looked at Mason for a moment, then they looked at Mimi, before they went on with eating their food, making no comment. But Mimi thought Jellyfish and Hawk were on to something. Mason *was* suppressing. He was ignoring his feelings and everyone else's. It didn't matter what past he had to bury or what emotions he denied, no one and nothing was going to get under that cowboy's protective layer.

He was so well defended from pain that he would likely never make the self-discovery his brothers had. It was going to be his way or no way. The new sheriff had a head of concrete, as Crockett had noted. And Mason was determined that his heart be fashioned of the same material.

She looked over at Mason, completely understanding why he was who he was, and knew she was the same as he.

It didn't matter. She still loved him. Though a lot of good that would do her.

"I think I'll go to bed," she said, standing. "Good night, gentlemen."

She put her plate in the sink and went upstairs. Nanette was in a bubble bath, blowing bubbles. Mimi tied up her hair and sat next to the tub, smiling at her daughter.

"Hi, Mommy," Nanette said with a cherubic smile.

"I love you," Mimi said.

"I know," Nanette said. "Ms. Helga says I can have cookies after dinner."

"She's good to you."

Nanette stared at the colors in a bubble, the translucent opalescence catching her attention. She was secure because of all the people who loved her.

"Mimi, can I talk to you for a minute?" Mason asked from behind her.

Chapter Seven

Mason looked at Mimi with strangely serious eyes. She felt her stomach jump with nerves. "Do you want me to towel Nanette off and get her dinner first? I need to get the sand out of the tub. Then Annette needs her bath," she said, pointing to the little girl waiting patiently for her turn.

"I'll help you. Come on, Nanette," he said, lifting his daughter from the tub. "Let's get you dried off."

Ten minutes later, they had two previously sandy girls cleaned off and changed and sitting at the dinner table. Hawk and Jellyfish played cards, shuffling them with quick rat-a-tats of movement. Helga filled two little plates, grinning at the men's antics as they deliberately showed off their card skills.

"We learned a lot while we were on the road,"

Hawk said, grinning at his giant partner. "Jellyfish can really charm the ladies out of their secrets."

"Hmm," Mimi said, "maybe a conversation for another time."

They laughed, but Mason grabbed her hand, pulling her out onto the porch. "Now we need to discuss some things."

"All right," Mimi said, amazed by his sudden tenacity. She'd been in the house for a few days and he hadn't seemed to possess a great urgency to communicate with her.

"First of all," Mason said, "I did not tell Nanette that I was her real father. I was completely agreeable to the two of us telling her together. In fact, I thought that was the right thing to do." He watched Mimi's expression. "She surprised me. She called me Daddy and I...I couldn't deny it."

"It was time," Mimi said softly. "I only wanted us to tell her together so that she'd be less traumatized or confused. Apparently, she is neither, and knows exactly who you are." Mimi smiled. "I'm glad."

Mason scratched his head under his hat. "I am, too."

"Is that all you wanted to talk about?" Mimi wasn't certain she could stand any more heart-to-heart with Mason. It wasn't a part of their relationship she was comfortable with now that they were at odds.

"Part of me thinks it's better that you're living in my house," Mason said. "A big part of me believes you're doing the right thing."

Mimi frowned at him. "I'm never going to be separated from my daughter."

"I wasn't implying that," Mason said hastily. "I was trying to figure out how we could make this less awkward between us. Housemates should have a reasonable amount of comfort around each other."

"No," Mimi said, feeling somewhat shattered that Mason thought he had to *try* to get along with her. "My comfort level's fine."

"Oh." Mason looked at her. "Sometimes I miss our old friendship."

Mimi nodded. "I know what you mean."

He smiled. "You do?"

"Yes. I think to get it back, you need to let Nanette and me move back to our own little house."

He shook his head. "That's not what I had in mind."

"What did you have in mind?" Mimi was amazed at the depth of thought Mason was expressing. "It's hard to get something back once it's gone."

"Yeah." Mason shifted. "I suppose that no matter what, our friendship has changed."

Mimi nodded. "I'm sure you're right."

"So since the old friendship can't come back, I

would like for us to work on making Nanette's childhood as normal as possible."

"I'm okay with that. In fact, I'm grateful that you're so interested in getting along with me."

"I am. Mimi," he said, his gaze narrowing on her, "why did Jellyfish say he'd marry you if he was more the settling kind?"

"I don't know. Jellyfish can be very random. You know that. His mind is always working."

Mason put big hands on her shoulders. An instant feeling of security swept over her as she stared at the Jefferson acres and felt this strong Jefferson man behind her.

"I think he has the right idea, but the wrong man. *We* should get married, Mimi."

Mimi's eyes widened. She was so thankful that Mason couldn't see her expression. The words she had waited what seemed a lifetime to hear!

"For Nanette's sake," he continued. "It would be best."

Mimi frowned slightly, perplexed.

"You and I know we can get along under the same roof. There's no reason not to have a united front. It will make everything better for Nanette, now and in the future. If there was anything you and I had in our corners growing up, Mimi, we had our fathers."

Was he proposing marriage—or a marriage of brave faces?

Whatever it was, it didn't sound like what she'd been dreaming of.

She turned to him. "Is that with separate bedrooms or without?"

"Oh, well," Mason said with a grin, "if you want sex written into the agreement, I can accommodate."

Walking back inside, she grabbed her purse.

"Where are you going?" Mason demanded.

"Out," Mimi said. "I need some fresh air."

He frowned. "Do women usually need air when they've been asked to marry a man?"

"As far as I can tell, you're not offering anything to get excited about," Mimi said. "You're just trying to keep your life as uncomplicated as possible."

"Hang on," Mason said. "I was trying to be more sensitive to my family. I was even trying to be perceptive."

Mimi turned toward him angrily. "Mason, you have no powers of perception. Hawk and Jellyfish are wrong."

She left, heading toward Calhoun's house.

Mason caught up to her. "Listen, I know I'm not the world's most softhearted guy. I don't do candy and flowers. But I'm willing to give our family a chance." He touched her arm. "Mimi, I think it would be good for everyone involved."

Mimi held her breath. Was she being selfish? What he was saying—if she looked at it unemotionally—made sense. She'd waited years for Mason to want to marry her. But she also wanted him to want her—and what it sounded like right now was that he wanted the marriage without the trimmings of true love.

"I never tried to trap you with sex, Mason," she said, her real feelings pouring out. "Frankly, I don't need a marriage to feel like I'm doing my best for Nanette. Sex? That was just something that happened between us. We blurred the lines of our friendship." She took a deep breath. "I think it would be a mistake to blur the lines of marriage with an uneasy truce. Let's not have any more confusion."

He stared at her. "I didn't feel like you tried to trap me with sex, Mimi, and if you took my pained joke a moment ago as a reference to that, then I apologize. If anything, what we shared that night was a golden opportunity to trap *you*."

She looked at him askance, not trusting her ears. "What do you mean?"

"Well, I'm standing here. I'm proposing. Most importantly, I'm the father of our child." His expression was fierce and protective, a side of him Mimi had never seen before. "Think about it, Mimi. You and I—" he caught her hand to his heart "—we have a hell of a lot of history between us."

She was so astonished she didn't know what to say.

After a moment, he dropped her hand and walked away.

THE THING MASON had always appreciated the most about Mimi—besides her steadfast friendship—was her unpredictability. For once, he wished she were more predictable. Just when he thought he'd finally figured out a practical way to avoid getting his heart more involved than it was, she turned him on his head again.

Only this time it hurt. In fact, it was not just his head. His heart stung with the ache of rejection. He'd heard his brothers babble over the years about how painful falling in love was—all of them had gone to great lengths to proclaim their "wounds"— but nothing, absolutely nothing could be as painful as finally dredging up a proposal and having your woman look back at you as though you were crazy.

A woman was supposed to cry happy tears and drag her man down to the jewelry store for an engagement ring. Or do something romantic like make a ring out of straw to seal the deal until the real thing could be procured.

But Mimi had stared at him, silent and apparently confused. It was disheartening, especially since he wanted so much to give his daughter what he'd had, which was a whole family. Sure, he hadn't had a whole family his entire life, but his early years, he remembered, were pretty darn secure.

Then there was the matter of his father's journal, which he didn't intend to read, but which brought him mixed emotions of pain and gladness. It provided security, and the knowledge that one day he could look forward to his father's thoughts and words, coming so many years after Maverick had left.

Security counted. Mason wanted Nanette to have it. Deep inside, he'd wanted Mimi to chase him a little, to show him that she knew that she wanted him. He was still stinging a bit that she'd married Brian. She had so much energy; he wanted her to use some of that energy discovering he was the only man for her.

True to her nature, Mimi had not chased. If anything, she'd become more aloof, he thought, striding into his house. More *friendly,* which was the death knell for romance as far as he was concerned.

"Hey," Last said, as Mason walked into the house. "I'm heading down to Calhoun's. The kids are already there. He's going to have a marshmallow toast outside. You wanna go?"

Nanette was going to roast her first marshmallow without him? Mason hesitated, even as his mind was in a dither about Mimi's nonacceptance of his very generous offer.

"You look tired," Last said. "Fatherhood tuckering you out?"

"No," Mason said with a glare. "Don't get started about how old dads need their sleep, either."

Last grunted. "Okay, Pops."

"I've got a lot on my mind," Mason snapped.

"You always do, Mason." Last looked at him. "Anything I can help with?"

"Actually, I think you can." Mason sighed. "Let's walk down to the marshmallow toast, and I'll tell you everything."

They headed out the front door. Last could help Mason make a decision about the journal. Last was also an excellent person to wheeze to about Mimi.

"Hawk and Jellyfish made a find while they were gone this time," Mason said. "They brought back a journal Dad had been keeping when he stayed up north."

Last stopped in his tracks. "A journal? How? What kind?"

"I don't know exactly. I haven't read it. I don't want anybody else to know until I've had a chance to read it. Then I'll decide the proper way to pass it around."

"No," Last said. "That's not right. You had to protect us when we were young, but now you don't make decisions for any of us anymore. You make decisions for the family ranch, with all of us in council. We should all read the journal at the same time. Good or bad, it's the only way it should be done."

Mason nodded with satisfaction. "You're exactly right. We'll pick a time in the near future. Soon. We'll make sure we have babysitters and schedule a few hours to see what Dad had on his mind."

"Man, that's weird," Last said. "Dad leaving a journal, and you talking about needing a babysitter all in one breath. Every day brings a new surprise, doesn't it?"

Mason grunted. "That brings me to my other topic of discussion. I proposed to Mimi."

Last stopped, then began pounding him happily on the back. "That's great!"

"No, it's not," Mason said. "She didn't accept."

Last raised a brow. "Mimi didn't accept?"

"No. She just stood there and stared at me. I felt pretty stupid, actually."

Last rubbed his chin. "Usually women are not

silent about proposals. It's either yes or no. Smiles or tears. Or they run away. But that's rare."

"Mimi would never run away," Mason said, but the thought made him worry. No, as long as he had Nanette, Mimi would stay close by.

"So what kind of brotherly advice do you want?"

"Well," Mason said slowly, "I think it would be best if she accepted."

"I see." Last raised an eyebrow. "And did you tell her that?"

"I think so," Mason said. "I'm certain I stressed my thoughts on that subject very clearly."

"I think I'm beginning to see some of what's going on," Last said. "When you proposed, did you have a ring?"

"No."

"It's not entirely necessary," Last said kindly, "but sometimes it does help make your point more emphatically."

Mason shrugged. "The idea came upon me on the spur of the moment."

"And did your proposal go something like, 'Mimi, I think it would be best if we got married for Nanette's sake?'"

"I probably said something like that."

"Did you say anything about the color of her eyes?"

"Hell, no," Mason said. "Mimi knows what color her eyes are." He looked at Last with a frown. "If that's the best advice you can spoon out, I'm in a big bowl of trouble."

"Not to be too personal, but by chance, did you tell her you loved her? Adored her? Anything that might derive from the Latin noun *amor?*"

"I approached it in a calm, rational, levelheaded manner," Mason said. "Unlike the rest of you, who either needed to fall out of a tree or a hang glider or a hot air balloon to figure out marriage might be your bandage."

"Yeesh," Last said, "let's keep walking. This one's gonna be tricky, and I don't want to miss the toasting."

Mason grimaced. The only toasting he had felt lately was when he was in bed with Mimi the other day. Then old feelings had simmered to the surface, making him realize he had more interest than he'd been allowing himself to remember.

Just thinking about it made him heat up.

"Bro, if I'd been Mimi, I don't think I would have taken you seriously," Last admitted.

That was the last thing Mason wanted to hear. "Well, there's sure nothing funny about a marriage proposal."

"Yeah, but it sounds like you offered it to her with about as much enthusiasm as you might have for boiled cabbage—not that I'm referring to Helga's cooking or anything."

"I like boiled cabbage!"

Last sighed. "I don't. I want my cabbage fresh, hot and sassy, if you know what I mean."

Mason rolled his eyes. "Only you could equate sex and cabbage."

"Dude, that's my point! If you were really in love with Mimi, and you really, really wanted to marry her, even something as simple as a lowly head of cabbage would take on a special glow."

"Last, you've finally lost me." Mason shook his head as he strode toward the fire pit where the kids were gathered. Several brothers, as well as Olivia and Valentine and Helga, overlooked the roasting with happy smiles.

Mimi didn't even look his way, Mason noted unhappily.

He wondered if Last was right. Perhaps Mason had been bland with his proposal. Mimi was a practical lady; his practical suggestion should have appealed to her. She wanted what was best for Nanette, as well.

Of course, Mimi had never been one to proceed along an average course. He watched her assist Nanette with a marshmallow and smiled. No matter

what, he sure was glad Nanette was his daughter.
He'd always loved her, but she was even more an
angel in his eyes now because she would forever
connect him to Mimi.

*I should tell her that. That's what Last thinks I
should say.*

He went and sat beside his new family. Mimi
looked at him, just a bare glance of greeting.

"Hi, Daddy," Nanette said. She handed him her
first roasted marshmallow, which he ate right from
her little fingers, to her great delight.

"Mmm," he said. "You're going to be a good cook
like your mommy."

"Yes," Nanette said, completely aware that she
was going to be just like her mother.

Mimi rolled her eyes at Mason. "Have I ever
cooked for you?"

"I have experienced some of your culinary skill."

"I don't remember," she said. "Probably nothing
more than sloppy joes."

"My favorite meal," Mason said.

That brought a slight smile to her face. "Anything
edible is your favorite."

Mason sighed. "A man has to eat."

Nanette handed him another marshmallow. "This
was a great idea," Mason said happily. "We just need

some hot dogs and sauerkraut, and life would be just about perfect."

Olivia looked up. "I've got some inside. Do you want me to get you one?"

Mimi giggled. "If you feed him, you'll end up feeding all of them."

"That's fine. Mason's been helping a ton around here." Olivia headed toward the kitchen.

"So," Last said, "do you have anything you'd like to share with the gathering, Mason?"

Mason stared at his brother. "No. I don't."

That only made Bandera and Fannin and Calhoun more suspicious. Which was part of the problem with having a large family—there were always more ears stretched out to hear your business.

"Tell us," Bandera urged.

"No." Mason glowered at him. He was still pretty sore with Bandera for not sharing Mimi's secret. Mason understood why Bandera hadn't, but still, a brother ought to be more loyal to his brothers.

The journal burned at the back of Mason's mind, and he sighed uneasily. "I do have something, but I'm not ready to share it right now."

"Is it…about the ranch?" Fannin asked, newly in from Ireland with his wife, Kelly, and their children. "Everything all right?"

Beside him, Mimi shifted, looking into the distance.

"Give us a topic at least," Calhoun said. "You're killing us, bro."

"Nah. Tonight is for marshmallows." He stood. "Mimi, could I talk to you for a minute? Alone?"

"Oh," the brothers and wives said in unison.

He could tell that embarrassed Mimi. "If you don't mind, folks, this particular family business is just between Mimi and me."

They all beamed and then tried to look as if they weren't, which none of them were successful in doing. Mason sighed. Mimi was reluctant to remove Nanette from her lap and follow him, and it didn't help to have his brothers gibing him.

Once she'd sent Nanette to sit with Valentine and Annette, Mimi rose to follow Mason. It was a beautiful evening, with twinkling stars as far as the eyes could see. The smell of the campfire teased his nostrils with memories of other marshmallow toasts and campfires, with Mimi always there, part of his life. And maybe a part he'd always ignored and never really understood.

It was said that sometimes someone had to lose something important before they fully realized its worth. He had been guilty of that, but now was the time to change. Never a man for change—God knows everyone ribbed him about that—now he wanted it desperately.

"Mimi," he said as they strolled toward the moonlit pond. Tex had been fond of planting lilies there; all the brothers had helped build a small swimming dock for the Jefferson children. The pond had been on Mimi's land, before he'd bought it, and the swimming hole had always been something that they'd shared.

Until she moved into town, away from him. That should have been his first wake-up call. Or second, or third.

"Mimi," he began again, when she didn't say anything, "I noticed you didn't answer when I proposed. In fact, it struck me that you seemed more shocked than…receptive." He took her hand in his and they walked onto the dock. During the day, it was shaded by a giant willow tree. Right now, under this beautiful, romantic willow tree, he intended to make everything right.

She looked at him, but there was no smile in her eyes. Mason's heart began thundering with foreboding. "It also hasn't escaped me that you still haven't replied to my proposal. It was an honest proposal, Mimi. I want you to know that."

She nodded. "I know, Mason. You are always honest."

"Not with myself," he said earnestly. "Mimi, you've changed my life by giving me Nanette."

Again, she nodded. "And I've thought a lot about that." Taking a deep breath, she said, "Mason, I called Brian today. After your proposal."

"Brian?" Mason's brows furrowed. "What does he have to do with this?"

"He's our family lawyer."

"Ours, too," Mason said, his heart beginning to take on a sharp case of heartburn. *Nerves,* he thought. *All men get nerves when their proposal is on the table.*

"I discussed with him what has happened recently," Mimi said, "that I had told you that you were Nanette's father. And that you had brought her to your house. Then proposed. In a rather sporadic, haphazard fashion for you, Mason. You've always been the most diligent thinker and deliberate decision maker."

She looked up at him, her eyes wide and clear. "You never asked me to marry you before. And then you took my child away from me. Your proposal has convinced me that the best thing for all of us…me, you, Nanette…is for me to move back to my town house." Her hand slipped from his. "If for no other reason than so we can remain friends and maintain some dignity between us, I'm filing for legal joint custody of Nanette."

Chapter Eight

Mason was shocked. His world bottomed out. Too many people had left him, and he wasn't about to give up the new little family who had come into his life. He told himself to be rational; he'd pushed Mimi too hard. *Take a deep breath, talk it out...* but before he could think of being more rational than he was, he grabbed Mimi to him and kissed her as if there was no tomorrow.

There *was* no tomorrow, based on what she'd just said. He kissed her until both he and she were breathless, and then when she stared at him, he kissed her again, desperate to hold her to him as long as she'd allow it.

God in heaven, don't leave me. I've just found you.

Mimi pulled away. "Mason!"

He commanded himself to calm down. "That's me. Somewhere under this hat."

"Have you totally lost your mind?" she demanded.

"I think so. If so, I probably should have lost it sooner. I feel great about it." She blinked at him, dumbfounded or maybe just as shocked as he was by the new him, so he picked her up in his arms.

"Put me down!"

"We have a choice. We can do this dry or wet. But we are getting into that canoe parked beside the dock, and I'm rowing you to the center of the pond until the sun comes up."

She shook her head. "Nanette."

"Will be fine with Aunt Olivia. Helga. Aunt Valentine. Aunt Kelly. In the boat you go, Miss Joint Custody."

"Mason, we could really talk about this on dry land," Mimi said, moving out of his arms and ungraciously into the canoe. "You've become as dramatic as all your brothers."

"That's probably a good sign," he said. "They've all changed for the better." He pushed off with a paddle and rowed smoothly toward the center of the pond, where he'd have her trapped under the velvet sky and diamond stars. He could be Mr. Romance as easily as any of his brothers!

"You're fine the way you are," Mimi said, a stubborn tone in her voice. "You shouldn't change."

"Becoming a father will do that to a man."

"You even kiss differently. I don't think that has anything to do with fatherhood," Mimi said, sounding annoyed.

"Mimi, I'm glad you're the mother of my child," he said magnanimously. He was about to say that she was a fabulous mother, and sexy as hell, but she splashed water on him with her paddle. Wiping his face, he contemplated the little woman across from him, all riled up with an opinion of some kind or another. Clearly he was hung for a sheep as much as a wolf, and there was nothing a man could do about that but be the wolf.

He rocked the canoe and dumped it, sending himself and a shrieking Mimi into the water.

"Mason!" Mimi squealed.

"Yes, my love," he said, sending her paddle spinning away through the water with his paddle. "Let me rescue you."

She began swimming away from him, calling him what might have been an impolite term for a donkey, so he caught her foot and dragged her toward him. He closed her mouth with his lips and silenced all those words she didn't mean.

To his surprise, she locked her legs around his waist. He dog-paddled for all he was worth, not about to give up the Mimi-lock. Damn, she felt good!

"We should have done this before," he murmured. "Too bad you're such an ornery lass."

"Smart aleck."

She tried to kick away from him, but he pulled her back with a laugh. "I like catching you," he said. "I only wish I'd known how much fun it was. I would have done this much sooner."

"Mason, this new you is…a stranger. I don't feel that I know you at all."

He kissed her lips tenderly, claiming them the way he'd always wanted to. "I'm Mason Jefferson, father of Nanette Cannady Jefferson, owner of a ranch, brother to many misfits, and best friend to a little blonde who always gets me into trouble. I call her Mimi-jinx, but not to her face."

With a squeal of outrage, she tried to pull away again. Laughing, he held her more tightly.

"Mason, let me go," Mimi said, giving him the slip as she swam away. He let her go, watching her as she hauled herself up on the pier. Tempted to pull her back in, he decided to give her a little rope to run with.

Glaring down at him, she said, "Don't expect me to help you haul that canoe back in. Nor find the paddles. Though if I did, I'd bean you with one."

Grinning, he swam to shore, then sat on the dock to empty out his boots. "Come sit by me."

"No!"

"We need to talk. Being contrary is all fine and good, but we need to get some things straight."

"I prefer to keep my distance. I can hear you just fine."

He shrugged. "No more custody talk. That's silly."

"Silly? I'm not going to live in your house anymore. And you're not taking my child away from me. That means we're going to need legal advice and agreements to keep us both happy." She wrung out her shirt and her hair. "To be honest, I thought it was generous of me to offer joint custody. I could ask for sole custody."

"Nah," Mason said, deciding to strip off his socks, roll up his jeans and go barefoot. "The court wouldn't grant you sole custody. You concealed my child from me all these years. Plus, I am the sheriff now, which would impress a judge," he said, polishing his badge with a careless sleeve. "You insisted, you know, on the sheriff bit."

She digested that in silence. Mason could feel her worrying about the custody issue, and that wasn't what he wanted. He could still taste her lips on his, and could remember the softness of her body as he'd held her. A hunger for her began to grow inside him, from a place he had long suppressed.

"Mimi, we don't need Brian. Not that I'm opposed to calling our favorite family legal beagle, but it's best if we work this out ourselves."

"Mason, you took Nanette and moved her over here. You specifically said she belonged at the ranch."

"Yes, and you do, too. I've done the right thing and proposed in order to make an honorable woman of you—"

She gasped. "Mason, I don't need you to make me honorable. I *am* honorable."

"Then let's make me honorable."

A sound like a sigh escaped her. "I'm moving back to my town house tonight. Decide what days you would like to have Nanette, be reasonable, and I'll tell Brian to hold off on the paperwork."

A chill settled over Mason that had nothing to do with the swim and his wet jeans. Mimi wasn't acting like the Mimi he knew. She had been a lot of things over the years, but he couldn't remember her being cool to him. Mason stood. "I still think Nanette belongs on her family ranch."

"Well, I don't, and I'm her mother."

"Proposal unaccepted."

"Of course!" Mimi stopped wringing things and put her hands on her hips. "I hate to tell you this, Mason Jefferson, but I'm not going to marry you just because I've had your child. I can think of no other circumstances under which I would want you *less*."

He frowned. "Well, how the hell am I supposed to fix things, then?"

"That's the point, Mason," Mimi said. "You *can't*." Then she walked away.

IT WAS HARD, OF COURSE. The hardest thing she'd probably ever do in her life was say no to Mason—about anything!—and then put a final wall of silence between them. But she'd loved him all her life, as a friend, as a man, and sometimes both. But he'd proved stubbornly resistant to loving her, and his proposal was not what her heart wanted to have him offer her because of Nanette.

That was pretty much like saying, "I think I'll eat because I'm hungry." Not, "I think I'll eat that rosy red apple over there because it's the most delicious-looking apple I've ever seen."

Temptation was not too much to ask for from the goddess of love. Mimi wanted Mason tempted by her, wanted him to want her because she was desirable and made his mouth go dry. "Big man, offering to marry me because he got me pregnant," she grumbled. "Some romantic love story that is!"

By the time they returned, the marshmallow

roasting was winding down. Mimi could see that Nanette was very tired, so Mimi thanked Olivia for holding Nanette and thanked Calhoun for organizing the sticks and gooey bits. Mimi took her daughter and carried her up toward Mason's house until Nanette sleepily insisted on walking. Then Mimi put Nanette in her truck and drove away from the ranch, wanting to escape before Mason could put up a big argument.

He didn't realize that she was serious. She was weak and filled with temptation of her own, so before she cracked and said yes, Mimi made sure she drove off. She didn't want her better judgment to be over-ruled by jumping into Mason's arms.

A very nice place to be, too, she thought sadly. When he'd held her in the lake and kissed her so fervently, a hairline crack had formed in her determination. This was how she'd wanted Mason all those years! Passionate, loving, exciting.

But she knew too well that he would settle quite quickly into the role of husband, and then ignore her as he pretty much always had. Not ignore her in a mean way, but once he didn't have to think about wooing her, he darn sure wouldn't.

The only way to know if Mason was looking for a bride or Nanette's mother was to test his "woo" gauge. If he wooed her, then he wanted her. "But if he keeps blabbing on about custody and Nanette and life at the family ranch, I'm going to give him a kick in the Jefferson jewels," Mimi muttered, glad that her daughter had fallen asleep again before the unruly thought escaped her lips. Mason and his responsibility issues were annoying!

If he did have these powers of perception Hawk had spoken of, they were deeply embedded. "I doubt he has them at all," Mimi said to her daughter, "and neither do you. You probably just thought he was your dad because he hangs around you more than any other man."

Wasn't it easy for a little girl to be confused about things like that? Mimi remembered playing imaginary games when she was a child—games wherein her mother returned. Her mother was a silver fairy, dressed in a shimmering gown, and she stayed home happily, baking apple pies and big dinners and sewing dresses for Mimi.

Mimi frowned. She didn't want Nanette to suffer those types of daydreams. If her daughter was wondering why her father was never around…that was a bad thing. Over the years, she had let the "father" issue go unaddressed, hoping Nanette's grandfather's presence would be enough to satisfy the little girl's paternal longings and questions until she was old enough to understand the real answer.

But there hadn't been a real answer, until Mimi had told Mason the truth. "Come on, sweetie," she said, parking the truck in front of her town house. "Let me get you inside to bed."

"Where's Daddy?" Nanette asked.

"He's at home, sweetie," Mimi said.

"Oh. Helga makes me sauerkraut and pancakes in the morning."

Mimi smiled as she helped her daughter up the stairs. "She has sauerkraut in our fridge, too. Don't worry."

"My stuffed animals are at Daddy's," Nanette murmured.

A shock went through Mimi. This was going to be harder than she'd thought. They'd need two of everything. It wouldn't work to send Nanette back and forth every other night—she'd get confused and unsettled. Once she started kindergarten, she'd need regularity with her schoolwork.

"Okay. We'll get them later. Right now, let's get you to sleep."

She put her daughter to bed, peeked in on her dad, and then went to her own room. Was she doing the right thing, being so stubborn about Mason? He had always been so many things to her. Loving him had never been easy. She put on a T-shirt, brushed her teeth and snuggled between the covers.

Her bed at Mason's had felt better, she had to admit.

What if they had made love before Calhoun opened the door? Would she feel differently about accepting Mason's proposal?

She would never know. All she did know right now was that she had dreamed for years of Mason wanting her enough to show it. But she wanted him to want *her,* not just Nanette.

A tap on her bedroom window made her squeal. It was Mason. In their childhood, Mason had not been averse to going around the sheriff's rules by tapping on Mimi's window.

"Mason," she said, after opening the window, "we do have a door."

"I knew your dad was asleep." He crawled off the tree branch and over the windowsill. "He needs his rest. Nice T-shirt."

It was an old shirt, one of Valentine's from her old days of working at the Never Lonely Cut-n-Gurls Salon. White, it had a purposely tatted bottom, with lettering that read *Save a Horse* on the front and *Ride a Cowboy* on the back. It was also very worn-out and comfortable.

"I don't need to dress in a baby-doll gown for my

dad and daughter," Mimi said crossly. "Besides, you've seen this before."

"I like it. Reminds me of a comfy old blanket." He sat on the edge of her bed, bouncing. "Let's go for a drive."

"Mason!" Mimi glared at him as he turned on a bedside lamp. Clearly, he hadn't come with seductive purposes in mind, and she wasn't certain if she was annoyed or relieved. "I can't go for a drive. Nanette might wake up and miss me."

"Then I'll just have to talk to you here." He pulled off his boots and made himself comfortable. "Where's the TV remote?"

"There's no TV, Mason. What's on your mind?"

"I called Brian." Mason looked at her, not interested in the lack of a TV at all. "I called him to discuss how best to handle custody, et cetera. Having never given up anything that is mine—not even my brothers, when folks thought maybe it was best to separate us after Dad left—I felt I should get his advice on the matter. Since he knows all of us and has worked for all of us, I knew he was probably ideal to guide me. I wanted to try to make this suggestion of yours as easy as possible on all of us, especially Nanette."

Mimi's chest tightened. Her whole world sinking, she knew exactly what Mason was going to say.

"Brian says you never called him about any custody questions, Mimi. And your little lie makes me wonder what exactly it is that you want from me *this* time."

Chapter Nine

Mason waited for Mimi to tell him what he wanted to know. What else was there for them to discuss? He'd already proposed to her. He really had nothing else to offer. Ever since he'd learned about Nanette, he had tried his best to be a very present father. He'd been so scared—really, scared was the only word he could think of—when Mimi told him she was seeking custody arrangements.

But when Brian had been honest with him... Why would she tell such a terrible untruth?

He waited, his heart in more of a wringer than he could ever remember it being. She was so beautiful; she was so much a part of him, that he couldn't understand how his best part could hurt him so much.

"Mason, if you want the honest truth—"

"And I *do* want it," he said sternly.

"I did call." Her eyes were as sad as his felt. "Brian wasn't in. The recorder came on, and…I just hung up. Something told me that I needed to talk to you first before I did anything with Brian."

His chest eased a bit. "Inexcusable."

"I know. I'm sorry for that."

He liked that she didn't try to justify her actions. "No fighting over Nanette."

"I don't ever want to fight with you," Mimi said, her tone as sincere as he'd ever heard it. "Mason, I—"

He held up a hand. "Whatever it is, don't say it. I am admiring your forthright approach."

She blinked. "I'll say whatever I want, and you don't need to be a smart-ass."

True. He was being a bit of a bear, but what was Papa Bear supposed to do when his cub wasn't in his house where she belonged? "Mimi, you need to come back to the ranch."

Mimi shook her head. "It's very awkward for me."

He sighed. "Fine. We'll take turns being awkward. Scoot over." Sitting on the edge of the bed, he hung his hat on the lamp on the bedside table, and decided he liked seeing his worn hat over Mimi's girlie lamp.

"Mason, we *cannot* sleep like this," Mimi said. He ignored her and settled his head on her comfy white pillow. God, he was tired. He was tired of arguing, and he was tired of thinking about all the dilemmas a big family entailed, and he was definitely weary of being responsible for everything under the sun where the ranch and all its remote members were concerned. "Mimi," he said, his eyes drifting shut, "for once, I am not interested in your protests. I'm imagining myself in a big fluffy white oasis of clean sheets and softness, and you can be my most warm and round maiden of the sheets."

"Mason, take your arm off my waist," he heard Mimi say, but he didn't care. He held her tighter to him, and his last conscious thought was that he never wanted to spend another night without holding his little Mimi-jinx.

MIMI COULDN'T SLEEP AT ALL. She glanced at the clock, seeing the numbers glow 3:00 a.m. Something heavy was squashing her—Mason—his big, muscled frame encroaching upon her space and her person. She was on her side, and he lay against her back, his big, hairy leg resting on her most private area.

It was quite intimate. Somehow it felt right. Mimi didn't dare move because she didn't want Mason to wake up, but something hard at the base of her bottom let Mimi know he was as awake as she was.

"Mason," she said, "don't even think about it."

"Calhoun's not here," Mason said, snuggling into her. "We'd be undisturbed." He nipped her neck, giving her delicious chills all over her body. "You go back to sleep, Mimi. I'm not ready to make love to you. I'm not about to take any milk unless I get the cow, too. And until I hear you moo, I'm a free man."

Mimi wriggled out of his arms. In the darkness, she could barely make out the lines of his face, and only that much because of the glow of the digital clock. But she knew his gaze was watching her possessively. "I do not moo, Mason. I will never moo. However," she said, giving his chest a poke, "we can't sleep together every night. You're going to have to change those plans."

"I guess the sheriff wouldn't like it," Mason said.

"I wouldn't like it," Mimi said. "I don't want to play house with you."

"All we're playing is bed," Mason said, giving her a little bounce. "Unless you feel like going downstairs and making me breakfast, you can't really say there's anything serious we're playing."

She sighed. "I think you're going to go hungry unless you know how to fix your own breakfast."

He nuzzled her shoulder, right into the curve of her neck. "You're a hard woman to get along with,

Mimi Cannady. But I miss you when you're not around to bother me."

She sniffed. "So you're forgiving me so soon? That's not like you."

"Maybe I'm getting used to having you in the crook of my arm," Mason said, pulling her next to him. "Anyway, nothing you do surprises me. I'm relieved you were fibbing about joint custody."

"It wasn't really a fib," Mimi said, starting to get annoyed. "I had every intention. I dialed the number. It's just not so easy...but maybe tomorrow," she said, struggling for her pride.

"Nah," Mason said. "If you quit trying to be the bossy old hen, everything will go a lot more smoothly."

"As long as you're the farmer in charge of the coop?" Mimi said, tensing. "When I told you about Nanette, I didn't realize I was going to be adding another person to my life. I thought we'd stay pretty much on the same paths we'd been on."

"Are you complaining?" he asked, choosing that moment to feather some light kisses along her hairline. The tension left Mimi slowly. What he was doing to her felt so good!

"Loudly complaining," she said, and he laughed.

"Sure you are. I hear you. But every once in a

while, you get real quiet," he said, kissing her lips and drawing a sigh of pleasure from her that Mimi was almost embarrassed to hear herself release.

He knew her so well that it was ridiculously easy for him to push her pleasure buttons. The hard part was being in bed with Mr. Hardheaded Cowboy and keeping herself from being tempted beyond all control! She was only human after all, and a human who had been proven quite weak where Mason was concerned.

"Stop," she said, tearing her lips away from his and pushing against his chest. "I admit it, you're driving me wild. It feels vaguely sinful and terribly wonderful." She flopped onto her stomach, protecting her space. "So if you don't mind, I'm going back to sleep."

He chuckled. To her amazement, she felt the bed give, and realized he was leaving. Not daring to see what he was doing, she listened as he put on jeans and zipped them. A few more movements and rustling noises, and then he left her room and walked down the hallway.

A few seconds later, she jumped as he said, "I've given Nanette one of her stuffed animals she left at my house. I expect her back tomorrow night, and you, as well, Mimi. Or else I will be back."

"I'll nail the window shut," she said, which drew

a hearty chuckle from him, and then he left out the window. Mimi blinked in the darkness, somehow feeling abandoned. "We have a front door, you know," she said sourly. "You don't have to act like Tarzan, swinging on tree branches."

But Mason would do exactly what Mason wanted, she knew, and mostly, coming in and out of her window suited him just as well as a door. All the brothers had made use of any entrance and exit to the houses of girls they were pursuing. Why should Mason be any different?

Pursuit, Mimi thought with a start. Mason was pursuing her! Just the way she'd always wanted! Okay, maybe not the way she'd dreamed about, but he was pursuing her as the other Jefferson men had pursued their women!

She tingled all over thinking about it. But it was his heart that she wanted most of all. She'd waited all these years to get it, eventually giving up hope.

And Mimi held close to another secret, one she hadn't included in the truth she'd told Mason tonight. She longed for another child…with him. He had many times said he didn't want children, that he'd raised all his brothers and had no desire whatsoever for more raising to do. But when he'd found out about Nanette, he'd realigned his position to include raising his daughter. And he *had* mentioned another child on the day they hadn't made love....

He was a good father. Such a good father, in fact, that a sweet kernel of desire for another one of Mason's babies had sprung to life inside Mimi's heart.

I want him. I want his love. I want to share his life, and I want him to tell me he wants our family to grow.

Then she would know that he was marrying her for her—and not just because he was determined not to be a deserting father. This way of thinking was dangerous territory, she knew, but it was the only territory she wanted to claim as her own. House was not a game she was interested in playing. It was all or nothing. And since she'd already had nothing with Mason, she could easily hold out for all.

No matter how sexy his kisses.

MASON GRINNED as Sheriff Cannady came into his office. Since it was Sunday afternoon, and not much was happening in town, there was probably only one reason Mimi's father was coming to visit him, and it wasn't to see his old office.

"Hello, Sheriff," Mason said, standing to shake his hand. "Sit down and tell me how life's treating you."

The sheriff sat, but he really didn't smile. "Life's good. Can't complain. Helga's making me eat lacto-fermented cabbage and health foods, and I have to go see a woman who gives me a special rubdown once a week. She's a big girl, like Helga, and I don't dare tell her no. Helga claims it's all beneficial to my liver. Mimi agrees with everything Helga says, so I'm starting to be more pliable about it."

Mason grinned. "I only get the cabbage treatment."

"You wait," Mimi's father told him. "One day, there'll be no more carrot cake for you. You'll get ginger tea for dessert instead."

Mason laughed. "She's a gold mine."

The sheriff looked at him, then kicked his boots up on his old desk. "So last night, I was getting some winks in, and I heard a strange noise. Sort of like a window going up, and then boots dropping on the floor." He pinned a gimlet gaze on Mason. "Strangely, I never heard the doorbell ring, nor the front door open."

Mason raised his eyebrows and said nothing, realizing the sheriff had decided to get on with the topic he'd come to discuss.

"So I was thinking about this, seeing as how I really enjoy nighttime visitors," the sheriff said. "I was thinking how much sheriffing meant to me over the years. Maybe I would have been nothing in life, but this town elected me to be sheriff, and I hung on to that faith the people had in me, even when I was real sick. Damn near died, you know, but I wouldn't surrender my badge."

"No, sir, you didn't." Mason nodded. "Mimi was real proud of your spunk."

The sheriff scratched his head. "See, and that's the funny thing. I thought my daughter would take my spot. Mimi would be a good sheriff, you know. She loves everybody, and everybody loves her. But she's tough as nails, by golly, and wouldn't think twice about spitting in the eye of the meanest bull on the planet."

Mason laughed. "She's run us all ragged over the years, Sheriff. No end to the excitement she brings to life."

"Yep." He nodded, satisfied with the compliment. "So I was thinking about that window and those boots and I'm thinking about how we live in town now. It's not like living out on our ranch, you know. Not nearly so much privacy. Tons of social occasions, and it's great to be close to Valentine's bakery, but no privacy. If you know what I mean." His stare was pointed.

"Ah, I think I'm getting your meaning," Mason said slowly.

"It's only because of what the badge meant to me," the sheriff said. "Respect. It's a helluva lot of respect the people of Union Junction give their sheriff. I think there comes a time when fun and games must go by the wayside." He pointed at a picture on the wall of himself as sheriff with several prominent townspeople. "Perhaps it's hard to respect a sheriff who shinnies up trees and sneaks in windows to get to a lady's bedroom."

Mason nodded. "Yes, I do see your point."

The sheriff stood. "Well, I hope you do. As I say, we really enjoy our visitors at the town house. In fact, you might even say that a certain sheriff is a great favorite in our home."

Mason nodded. "But you'd prefer the sheriff to use the front door."

Sheriff Cannady held up his hands as he walked to the door. "Or the back door, son, it doesn't matter. We're not particular in the Cannady household. Door, not window, is all we ask. For the sake of the badge. And…for my daughter's reputation. People would be expecting me to get a shotgun after a man sneaking into my daughter's bedroom, you see. And I haven't got a shotgun or any firearms anymore. Not since Nanette came into my life. Not safe around children, you know."

Mason looked at the sheriff. Nanette had brought a lot of changes to everyone's life. He knew how much a grandchild had meant to Sheriff Cannady. "Appreciate you coming by, Sheriff."

"Good visiting with you…Sheriff," he said. Then he nodded. "You boys are like sons to me, Mason."

Mason smiled. "I know. Thanks."

The sheriff left, his shoulders straight and proud, and Mason knew he was looking at one of the finest men he'd ever known. "Door, not window," he murmured, trying not to smile.

The sheriff was absolutely right. Mason needed to respect the badge, and Mimi, and the sheriff himself. Which meant he was going to have to find another way to sneak up on Miss Mimi. She was known for keeping doors tightly shut.

He was shocked when she stepped inside his office just then, like really good karma. "Hey," he said. "Your dad just left."

"Oh?" Mimi's eyebrows rose. "What was he doing here?"

Since he could tell she honestly had no idea about her father's request, Mason decided to avoid raising the issue and see what she had on her mind. "Reminiscing over his old office," Mason said.

Mimi nodded. "The only reason Dad's been able to completely give up being the sheriff is because you took the job. He thinks you'll make a good one."

"If I put away my childish ways," Mason said.

She frowned.

He grinned. "Come here and sit in my lap. You make me happy just looking at your pixie face."

She shook her head. "We have important things to discuss."

"Oh. Important things. Well, that sounds…important."

"It is," Mimi said earnestly. "Mason, you can't sneak in my window anymore."

"And you can't keep my daughter away from me. Which you have known since you told me about her." He frowned at her. "Mimi, I am not a second-rate dad. I didn't have one, and you didn't have one, and our child is not going to have one. It's not my way."

"Maybe there's a solution," she said.

"Excellent," Mason said, thinking they might be getting somewhere with the marriage proposal.

He got up, closed the door and locked it. "Your father wants me to respect the badge," Mason said softly. "And you."

Chapter Ten

Mimi's blood tingled as she looked at the hooded expression Mason wore. Why had he locked the door? "Dad is very protective of everything," she said, trying to sound normal.

"So am I," he said, picking her up and sitting her on top of his desk. He kissed her neck and ran his hands underneath her skirt.

Mimi's heart raced. "I just think everything should be out in the open."

He slipped down the straps of her spaghetti top. "I agree." His hands cupped her breasts, and Mimi realized talking was not on Mason's agenda. She tried to slide off the desk, but he moved between her legs, holding her prisoner.

"Mason," she said on a gasp, trying to fight the

tingling flashing through every sensual part of her body, "what does this have to do with our discussion?"

Warm fingers pulled her panties down and began a tantalizing dance on her most private area. All thoughts of her battle plan flew into disarray. Moaning against Mason's shoulder, she caressed the strong muscles of his back. "I do respect you, Mimi Cannady, even if you drive me nuts."

She couldn't think for the magic of his touch. This man—she had loved him all her life. First as a best friend, then as more. Nuzzling his neck, Mimi undid his belt buckle and jeans. "I respect you, too," she said, "but you drive me nuts."

His low chuckle tautened her nipples. He was so sexy, so powerful, so manly! She breathed in his scent. There was never going to be another man like Mason, and her heart knew it, as well as the most feminine part of her body. So when he pulled her forward onto his heat, she wrapped her legs around him and held on for dear life as he rocked into her.

"Oh, God," she said on a groan that came from deep inside. "*Everything* about you feels so good."

He suckled her breasts, and she tried not to scream because it was a public building, but when his hand slid between them to tease her hotly, Mimi couldn't help the sound that ripped from her. Mason groaned, gripped by her unbridled pleasure, which sent her over the edge again. "Mason!" she gasped.

Deepening their connection, he cried out his own release against her lips, sending chills of joy and secret pride into her heart. Mimi knew right then that four years had been too long to wait to be with the man of her dreams.

Four years was too long to wait for sensual heaven.

THIRTY MINUTES LATER, Mason had talked a flustered Mimi into leaving the sheriff's office. She was convinced that everyone in the town knew what she'd done on a Sunday, in her father's old office.

He laughed at her and tugged her outside. "I hope you're proud of yourself," he said, "taking me away from my duties."

"I am," she said, "if somewhat embarrassed."

"Don't be. Every sheriff should have his future wife christen his office in such a manner."

"Now, Mason," Mimi said, stopping on the sidewalk not far from the Union Junction Salon. "Let's not get crazy."

He laughed. "Mimi, over the years, it was me saying that to you. Remember when you talked me into sending that silly e-mail to Julia about a housekeeper, and it brought all the stylists out to my house?"

Mimi frowned, which he thought was cute. He loved reminding her that she had a penchant for trouble.

"That's not what I meant, Mason. I am not your future wife. Not at this moment. I can't even think about that right now."

"After what we shared, you're thinking about marrying me, Mimi," he said mildly.

She gave him a glare. "Mason, you are not yourself. What happened to Mr. Methodical? Mr. Slowpoke?"

"He's ready to start a family, Mimi," Mason said cheerfully.

Mimi stared at him. "I never thought I'd hear you say that."

He shrugged. "Nanette needs a little sister or brother."

The look on her face was priceless.

"Mason, I don't even know you anymore," Mimi said, seeming lost by the admission.

"Did you think I wouldn't want more children?"

"Well," Mimi said, "you always said you didn't want a big family. That you'd raised enough kids."

"Yeah, but…I'm done now. My boys are all gone. I don't have to be father-big-brother-uncle-teacher-coach anymore. I can walk my own path." Grinning, he swept her into his arms, right in broad daylight, which surprised her into compliance. That was what

Mimi needed, more surprise and less room to maneuver her own thoughts, he decided. "My dad had twelve," he said.

Gasping, she wriggled down out of his arms. "Mason Jefferson, you are a corn-fed bull if you think I believe you want twelve children."

"From this day forward, I am making love to you every single day," he promised. "Let's see how many we can make."

She shook her head, obviously stunned. "You're crazy."

"Nah. Just happen to think twelve's a great number when it comes to children."

"And here I was thinking that the idea of children would put you off," Mimi said. "I'll have to find another way."

"To put me off marriage? Why? You've tried so hard all these years to catch me."

He loved watching her suck in her breath with indignation. A grin broke out on his face that he couldn't have controlled if he wanted to.

"I did *not* try hard to catch you, Mason. It's just amazing that head of yours can fit inside your hat." She twirled and went down the street, her feet marching her stubbornly toward the Union Junction

Salon. Mason grinned wider. She'd be back—and it would be on his terms this time.

He was going to romance that little girl until she finally realized that she was his—and if he'd started a little slow in the romance department, according to Last, well, then that just meant the best times were ahead of him.

But when he went to her house that night, holding a bouquet of wildflowers he'd picked himself, and the sheriff opened the front door for him, Mason learned an uncomfortable lesson about a woman whose stated desire was to escape the marriage noose.

"She's gone, son," Sheriff Cannady said. "She and Nanette are staying in the Union Junction Salon. They had a room available, you know, since Lily got married."

Through his shock, pain and anger, Mason told himself to stay calm. Mimi was an easily frightened filly, who needed a gentle hand to lure her to his will.

Actually, Mimi was a spirited filly who was determined to do as she damn well pleased, and hang whatever he thought. Mason felt his jaw clenching and told himself to relax. "I'll go scout her out."

"I'd wait a bit, Mason," the sheriff said kindly. "Sometimes you can lead a horse to water, but you can't make it drink. I think she needs a little time to clear her head."

Mason shook his head. "She's had all the time she's getting, sir." He pinned his badge on Sheriff Cannady's chest. "Just to make sure I don't disrespect the badge."

MIMI TOOK A DEEP BREATH as she and Nanette looked around their temporary room. "This is beautiful, isn't it, honey?" She loved the feeling of being in a room meant for a woman, in a house of women.

For the first time in her life, maybe, Mimi felt herself relax. This was the vacation she needed. "It's better than a weekend at a spa," Mimi told Nanette, settling the little girl on the bed to tie her shoe.

"What's a spa?"

Mimi smiled. "It's a place to take a vacation and be pampered."

"What's a vacation?"

"Something I don't think I've ever taken you on." Mimi looked at her tiny, wonderful daughter. "You'll be in school in a few years. Let's enjoy this vacation, and then take another, before you get busy with your education."

Nanette smiled. "'Kay."

A rap on her door sounded. "Mimi! Join us for chocolate chip cake!"

"That would be Shasta, and most likely, Aunt Valentine is here with a yummy treat." Mimi patted Nanette's hair, admiring the shine of it. Girl talk, treats and sleeping alone was just what the doctor ordered. After today's frantic lovemaking in Mason's office, Mimi knew Mason was going to drive her mad with desire.

He was tearing down every wall she put up.

It was too much, too fast, too soon, for a man who had been a stalwart bachelor. She didn't trust it. Head-over-heels desire didn't usually translate to a lasting relationship. Her mother was a good example of that, abandoning her family years ago.

And what if her mother's genes had come to her and the lure of wanderlust tempted her?

Mimi would never, ever leave her daughter, of course. She squeezed Nanette to her in an affectionate hug. But the past had very long tendrils into the present, as Mimi knew too well.

Mason claimed she was a smidge flighty. He called her Mimi-jinx, in a teasing way that said he meant the pet name.

What if her history meant she wasn't destined to be married? Certainly, she had chosen a platonic arrangement for her first marriage, which hadn't lasted and was never meant to.

"I love you," she told Nanette fiercely.

Nanette smiled. "Let's go eat cake, Mommy."

Cake. With friends. What more wonderful thing to take her mind off the sudden fear striking her?

Opening the door, she took her daughter's hand. "First one there gets the biggest piece," she said.

Nanette giggled and ran on steady, muscular legs down the hall. Mimi heard laughing voices and delight envelop her daughter as Nanette ran inside the screened-in porch.

Sisterhood. Without Mason, Mimi thought, trying not to feel sad. *A vacation away from a handsome man. Right. And if you're pregnant now?* a laughing voice asked her, shocking her.

Now more than ever she wasn't ready to think about marriage, but if she was expecting a baby, Mason would be more determined than ever to make her Mrs. Mason Jefferson.

Her head felt suddenly light. She sank onto a flowered ottoman next to Nanette, who had been given a very generous piece of cake. But Mimi had no appetite.

"You look pale, Mimi," one of the women said. "Are you all right?"

"I think so." Velvet handed her a glass of water, which Mimi sipped gratefully.

"Hey!" Mason said, calling through the screen. "I didn't get an invitation to eat cake."

"Daddy!" Nanette said, jumping up and nearly spilling her cake. "You can share mine."

"Oh, no, cowboys get all the cake they want, honey. You're very sweet, though," Marni said. "I'll go let him in."

"Must be a social call," Gretchen said with a wicked smile, "since the shop isn't open."

Mimi felt a blush run up her cheeks. She sipped her water more urgently, trying to cool off her system.

To her surprise, Mason came in, kissed his daughter, said a brief hi to Mimi, and then sat down and ate cake, allowing all the women to spoil him as he no doubt thought his due. When he was done being petted like a pasha, he got up, thanked the ladies politely, kissed his daughter goodbye and left.

In the twilight, Mimi could hear him whistling as he walked down the main street of Union Junction. Mimosas wafted their perfume through the screens as she listened to his happy sounds.

"Where's he going, Mommy?" Nanette asked.

"Home to bed," Mimi said, feeling terribly guilty that she was keeping Nanette from her father. Was she? He hadn't seemed upset that they were here. "I'm a terrible mother," she said suddenly, not meaning for the words to leave her lips.

But they had, and instantly everyone gathered around her, hugging her and reassuring her, much as they had doted on Mason. *Okay, it feels good,* she thought. *So maybe he needs love and attention.*

Mason had never really had anyone who loved him and spoiled him and looked after him. Except Helga, but that wasn't the same. *And me,* Mimi thought.

He was trying to make her feel guilty, she realized. That was why he'd come here. It was working like a charm!

"I'm all right," she told the ladies. "Everyone enjoy their cake. I had a moment of sentimentality, but it's over now."

"We thought it had something to do with that fine cowboy, with his extra-fine buns packed into those jeans," someone teased. "Maybe you'd rather be going with him than staying here?"

"No," Mimi said. "I need this time to re-center myself."

"Pretty powerful stuff, is it? That Jefferson charm?"

The ladies all laughed, but Mimi didn't feel like it. She'd lost her best friend, in a way, as she'd feared she would. She didn't know Mason anymore, even less since he'd made love to her in his office. That had just confused matters between them. She wanted him, and yet, deep inside, something was warning her that it wasn't meant to be. And if she was pregnant?

Worry slithered down Mimi's spine. She felt smothered and out of control. She wanted to know what was real between them before they said vows that one day might be meaningless.

Her gaze fell on Nanette, happily finishing her cake.

It hit her before she could put a name to it: a sudden, terrifying desire to move as far away as she could possibly get from Mason Jefferson and his devastatingly sexy cowboy charm.

Before they made a mistake they'd both regret.

Chapter Eleven

Mason had intended to barge into the Union Junction Salon yesterday and drag his lady and his child back to the ranch where they belonged, but once he got there and saw the strain on Mimi's face, he knew the sheriff was right in kindly telling Mason to cool his jets.

Mimi looked tired and not her usual happy self. He was worried, because before, there had always been a special light in her eyes for him, as well as a smile and a twinkle in her personality. He missed that. He missed everything about her.

He missed making love to her. Now that his feelings had overcome his better judgment where Mimi was concerned, he was ready to throw better judgment completely out the window and make love to her every day of the week. Maybe every hour of the day.

I could get used to that, he thought with a smile.

"You look happy to see the sun rise," Last said, coming into the breakfast room where Mason sat with a cup of hot coffee. "Good news?"

"Nope."

"Must be the sauerkraut." Last helped himself to some coffee and sat down across from his brother. "Heard Mimi moved into the salon with the gals."

The smile slipped from Mason's face. "So?"

Last shrugged. "Just repeating gossip, Sheriff."

Mason's lips flattened into a straight line. "It's only temporary."

"That's what I thought," Last said with a nod. "Especially since she'd slept here one night, and one night at the town house—"

"What does it matter?" Mason demanded. "And does the whole town have to be in our business?"

"Yep," Last said. "You are the sheriff, bro."

"I keep getting reminded of that." Mason felt very sour about the interest his every move was attracting. "Can't a guy get to know the mother of his child?"

"Well, I think that makes folks a wee bit more interested in your business," Last said easily, "since nobody had any idea that Nanette was your daughter. I guess they're wondering what's next."

"Next?" Mason's brow furled.

"Well, maybe wedding bells," Last suggested.

"Clearly you and Mimi like each other enough to make a child together. Of course, it's none of my business." Standing, he went to the sink to rinse out his coffee cup.

Mason sighed. "Mimi won't marry me."

Last looked at him. "I've given you all the advice I had. Wish you the best of luck with it, though."

He left, and Mason's mood was not improved when Calhoun wandered in, grabbing himself a cup of coffee.

"Enjoyed the marshmallow roast," Calhoun said. "Think I'm going to cook hot dogs tonight. Shall I toss a few extra on for your clan?"

"My clan?" Mason demanded. "Do I look like I have a clan as I sit here by myself drinking a cup of coffee?"

Calhoun glanced around. "Mimi and Nanette not here?"

"You must not have the connection to the grapevine Last has."

"Probably not," he said cheerfully, plenty pleased to have it that way.

"Mimi's staying at the Union Junction Salon for a few days," Mason admitted.

"Huh." Calhoun drank his coffee down in one gulp. "Sounds like woman trouble, and I'm no good with that one. My woman keeps close tabs on me."

"Fine," Mason said, grumpy about the situation. Mimi wouldn't keep close tabs on him no matter what.

Shrugging, Calhoun left. Mason looked dolefully into his coffee cup. The brew was cold now, as cold as he felt, and brought him no pleasure whatsoever. He could rarely remember feeling that displeased about a cup of coffee.

It's Mimi. She's ruining my morning joe.

If she was here, where she belonged, she could fix him a cup of coffee, and he'd be so grateful that he wouldn't even need sugar in it.

Or maybe he'd fix her a cup of coffee, if she wanted.

He had no idea how to get her into his house, his life, his bed. The sheriff's desk incident had probably given her the clue that he had no self-control around her, and she'd stay well clear of him.

To his astonishment, Mimi blew into the kitchen just then. She sat down across from him and gave him a very serious glare.

"Mason Jefferson, you're ruining my reputation," she said.

His mouth curled. "I offered. You turned me down."

"Not that reputation," Mimi said. "My reputation for being sensible. Logical. Sane."

"Uh—" Mason gawked, wondering when anyone had ever thought Mimi was logical and sensible. But he dared not say such a thing, or she'd blow him clean out of his boots. "I'm not sure how to fix that," he said. "Can you give me a hint of what the exact issue is?"

"The issue is that everyone, including my dearest friends, thinks I'm not giving you a chance to be good to me."

He perked up. This topic sounded exactly like what he thought. "Maybe your dearest friends have a point. They know I've changed."

"Changed?" Mimi stared at him. "I liked the old Mason. Him I trusted. You," she said steadily, "are telling me you want to marry me, and you're trying to make me say yes by making love to me, but that's not love. It's lust."

"Lust works for me," Mason said. "I won't quibble about it. I hope I lust for my wife for the next thirty years, or until my pe—"

"Whoa," Mimi said. "What I'm talking about is depth of friendship."

"So? Who is a better friend to you than me?"

"Friends listen to friends' feelings," Mimi said. "You don't listen to me."

"Mimi, anyone who doesn't listen to you gets a purple ear from the pressure of your personality," Mason told her kindly. "Even mine are getting a bit pink around the edges."

She put her hands on her hips. "Well, let's test that theory. I'd like to start putting some money away for Nanette to go to college in Boston."

"No," Mason said automatically. "Nanette stays in Texas."

Mimi glared. "You see what I'm talking about."

"No, that's not a fair subject. Try another."

"All right. If we got pregnant again the other day—"

"During our burst of passion," Mason said, happily joining in. This topic he liked.

She sighed. "If we did, I don't want you pressuring me about marriage."

"Okay, you pressure me instead," Mason said. "I'll say no, secretly call the minister, and we'll pretend like we're not saying our wedding vows when we actually are. The moment will be over, and the drama past, and you'll have caught me fair and square. Only we'll never say that," he said with a grin. "We'll say we're positively aligned with each other's auras."

"Mason!"

He shrugged. "I just think you're being ridiculous. I like you, you like me, let's get married. Then it won't matter if we're pregnant again. And we'll only be on number two anyway, so we'll just be getting started."

"Why, Mason?" Mimi asked. "Why now? Why do you suddenly think that marriage is a good idea?"

He scratched his head. "I want my own clan."

Mimi wrinkled her nose. "Ugh. That's not very romantic."

"I don't do romance as well as I do steadfast," Mason said. "You could learn to like steadfast, I bet. If I can learn to deal with headstrong and flighty, steadfast can be something you decide you like."

"But you know," Mimi said, "we were such good friends. We'll never have that if we're married."

"We don't have it now," he pointed out. "All this chitchat is getting in the way of what could be a really satisfying time in our lives."

"You'd forget about me once we were man and wife," Mimi said.

"Fat chance," Mason said. "Do I look like I ignore naked women in my bed? I promise you, Mimi, you come to bed naked, and I will never, ever forget you. Or," he said thoughtfully, "you can keep that T-shirt you wear. Just nothing on underneath."

"I keep expecting you to whip out a contract," Mimi said. "This all feels so methodical."

"You think about it," he said, "and in the meantime, think about this."

He kissed her, making certain he lifted her clear

off her little sandals, holding her tightly. His lips held hers, and his tongue swept hers, and he knew he had her when he felt her go limp in his arms.

"I have to get to work," he said, "but I sure thank you for dropping by. A man should have a friendly smile to go with his cup of java." Tipping his hat, he left, feeling very satisfied with himself and the direction his love life was going.

It was the dawn of a new day, he thought, my way. Always he had let Mimi run things, and all they had to show for it was some memories of tying cans on goat tails and painting on people's barns.

From this day forward, Mason intended to make the plans for them. And the first plan he was going to make was one for a wedding.

"I KEEP TALKING about romance, and he keeps talking about marriage," Mimi told her friends at the salon. "As if it's something people can do in two minutes down at the local greasy spoon. I'll have a burger with that marriage," she said, mimicking Mason's deeper voice. "You can't short-order a meaningful relationship."

"Sex," Velvet said. "Sex makes a man think romantically."

"Pretty sure we've researched that a bit," Mimi said, hedging.

"But romantic sex," Marni said. "That's what separates the women who get what they want from the women who don't."

Mimi blinked. She wasn't sure if sex in a field and sex in an office qualified as romantic. Their entire lives, she and Mason had been together twice. "Maybe I don't have the concept of romance."

Her friends laughed. Mimi felt herself blush.

"Handcuffs," Gretchen said.

"No," Mimi said. "He may be sheriff, but he is not going to put me in handcuffs. Although he'd probably like it," she said. "He has a caveman personality sometimes."

Giggles made her blush again. "Come on, girls, Mason was my only love. There's never been anyone for me except him. Handcuffs—no."

"Girls, we have an important job to do," Violet said. "Get out the good book."

They all laughed, and Shasta went to a closet. She pulled out a giant red feather-bound book. "We know what we want when we finally find the right thing," she said. "So we compiled a cookbook, you might say. *Cooking Between the Sheets,* by the Union Junction Salon sisterhood."

Mimi gasped. "You smart things!"

"It has our best recipes, and our best romantic

ideas," Carly said. "What we'd like if we meet someone special, and what we think a woman can offer her man."

"Sounds like what I need," Mimi said. "I've been worried that I'm too much like my mother to settle down, but I think what I really am is afraid."

"The man-woman thing is scary," Dixie said. "Here."

She handed the feather-covered book to Mimi.

She slowly opened the book, clapping it closed when they heard the front door open. "I bet that's Mason bringing Nanette," she said. "Please hide the book!"

Daisy took it and slid it neatly under the ottoman cushion. But it was Delilah who walked in, and, grinning, Daisy pulled the book back out again.

"Hi, Delilah!" they all said.

"Working, I see," their former boss said with a smile. "Creative juices flowing?"

"We're showing the book to Mimi," Kiki said. "She'd like a little inspiration, and we thought we'd test-drive it on her."

"It worked for me," Delilah said with a twinkle in her eyes. "Jerry and I thought we'd had all the romance we could stand. But now," she said, laughing, "even watching a movie in bed is not the same."

The ladies clapped, and Mimi tried not to be completely embarrassed. Delilah gave her a hug.

"I heard a rumor that you told Mason about Nanette," Delilah said. "And that he accepted the news with great joy and excitement."

"Yes." Mimi nodded. "He has a fathering bone I never knew existed in his body. He always said he didn't want children of his own, but I think something's gotten uncorked. Even the thought of having a big family seems enticing to him now."

Delilah smiled. "I'll bet getting all his brothers married off took quite a load from his shoulders. Here. I brought you something."

Mimi took the silver-and-white shopping bag Delilah handed her. "A present?"

"Something to celebrate the occasion," Delilah said, sitting on the ottoman by Mimi. "Having a child is a wonderful experience for a man, but I suspect I know Mason well enough to know where his next thoughts will be turning. So, I appointed myself your surrogate mother and I went and bought you something I think you'll need. Every mother should have the chance to buy one of these for her daughter for the big day."

"Big day?" Mimi asked, pulling the silvery tissue from the bag to find an airy, twinkling, baby-doll nightgown. "Oh, my," Mimi said, laughing nervously. "I've never seen anything so beautiful."

Her friends laughed. "Hold it up, Mimi," someone said, and when she did, the lace was so sheer as to be bare except for the pretty sequins.

"A wedding nightgown," Remy said.

"Or a nightgown to make a man think about weddings," Tisha said, and everyone agreed.

"Did I hear something about weddings?" a male voice asked.

Chapter Twelve

Mimi shrieked and hid something. Mason grinned, realizing he'd stepped in on something. "Can I see?"

"No!" Mimi exclaimed.

"Mason," Delilah said, hugging him, "you are like a child opening a gift. No, you cannot peek. But it sure is good to see you."

Mason returned Delilah's hug. "Where's Jerry?"

"Hauling to Missouri. He'll be back soon."

Nanette burst into the room and into Mimi's arms. Mason grinned. "She was checking out the puppies in back. You ladies rescued a new dog?"

"Six baby bird dogs," Shasta said. "The owner is elderly and couldn't keep them. She didn't realize her dog was expecting when she took her in off the street."

"Can I have a puppy, Daddy?" Nanette asked.

Mason's and Mimi's eyes met. The room fell

silent. This would be the first time a co-decision would be made over anything concerning Nanette.

Of course, Nanette was his princess and he instantly wanted to say yes. But he felt the right thing to do would be to let Mimi answer the question that had been addressed to him.

"Why don't we discuss it later with your mother?" he said reasonably, and the tension in the room lightened automatically.

Mimi smiled at him.

"Good choice, Dad," Kiki said, walking past him.

He felt real good about jumping that major hurdle.

"What are these?" Nanette asked, holding up a pair of pink feather handcuffs.

Mason's and Mimi's gazes met again, and this time Mimi's eyes were wide. Perhaps even guilty, he thought with amusement. Handcuffs? For him? He sure hoped so.

"Nanette, why don't we go visit Aunt Valentine at her bakery," he said, taking pity on Mimi. She had blushed the color of a near-ripe strawberry. "We'll see you when you're done in here, Mimi."

They left, Nanette's hand in his, but Mimi's expression told him a lot. She was up to something again, and he couldn't wait to see what it was.

Five minutes later, Valentine smiled when they

walked inside her bakery. "How do you always know when I'm just about to take cookies out of the oven?"

"Good timing," Mason said. "Smells like chocolate chip."

"You get a prize. Come on, Nanette. Let's show your father how to take cookies out to cool."

"Believe me, some things I can figure out on my own." But he followed, anyway, happy to be getting a treat. They sat at the table in the back, and Mason grinned at the tasty cookies on the plate in front of him and Nanette. "Mmm. Aunt Valentine's is always a good place to come hide out, isn't it?"

Nanette nodded, already choosing a couple of cookies.

"So, what's Mimi up to that you're needing to hide?" Valentine asked.

"Not sure. The ladies were having some kind of tea party, I think, and they weren't expecting us." He grinned. That was an understatement.

"What were those pink feather things Mommy had?"

Mason blinked.

"Pink feather things?" Valentine asked. "That sounds saucy."

It was Mason's turn to feel some heat on his face.

"Nanette, honey, I think those were something for the puppies," he fibbed.

Valentine laughed. "I know exactly what pink feather things you're talking about. It sounds like Mimi's planning a new kind of adventure. Maybe a romantic one."

"Yeah." He knew Valentine was teasing him, and he didn't really mind. But he hoped Mimi was planning something that included him.

"So, have you and Mimi ever dated?" Valentine asked.

"Dated?" His mind spun as he tried to think of all the things he and Mimi had done over the years.

"You know, that thing two people do who are interested in each other?"

The front doorbell tinkled. "Sorry I'm late," Mimi said, walking into the room. "Hi, Valentine. Hi, Mason."

She didn't look at him. That was a bad sign. Most women smiled at him and tried to flirt with him, even if it was harmless flirting. Trust Mimi to be different.

"What's in there?" Mason asked, pointing at the silver-and-white bag Mimi held.

"Nothing," Mimi said, holding it to her side so he couldn't peep at the "nothing." Mason decided that whatever it was, it wasn't meant for his eyes. If they were married, Mimi would be more comfortable around him, he was certain. He wanted to know every little thing about her. He knew a lot about the girl he'd grown up with, but almost nothing about the woman she'd become.

Dating. Valentine might have hit on the only way to get Mimi to loosen up around him and discuss marriage without getting that wild-colt look in her eye.

They claimed he was a man who didn't change easily, who was stodgy and stuck on his saddle. But he could change just as easily as anyone else—if it was the appropriate thing to do.

"Mimi, would you like to go out tonight?" he asked.

She stared at him and clutched her shopping bag to her more tightly. "Go out?"

He smiled reassuringly, feeling positive vibes coming from Valentine. "On a date."

"What's a date?" Nanette asked.

"It's when a man wants to spend time with a woman he likes, honey," Mason said.

"I can watch Nanette," Valentine offered.

"What kind of date?" Mimi asked, doubt in her pretty blue eyes.

"A surprise date," Mason said, because he hadn't planned that far.

"I like surprises," Nanette said.

"Me, too," Valentine agreed.

"All right," Mimi said.

"I'll pick you up at seven," Mason said, realizing he'd never said anything like that to Mimi. This was easy! Easy as getting thrown from a bull. He had this romance stuff in the bag. All the crowing and complaining he'd listened to from his brothers over the years had clearly been drama.

Getting up, he tipped his hat at both the women, and kissed his daughter goodbye. He wanted to kiss Mimi, too, but tonight he would kiss her all he wanted.

"WHAT WAS THAT ALL ABOUT?" Mimi asked Valentine when Mason had left.

"I don't know." Valentine shrugged. "Cookie?"

"I'd better not, since Delilah wants me to wear this one day." She pulled the dreamy baby-doll nightie from the tissue.

"Wow!" Valentine admired it, touching a finger to the sequin-covered straps. "You'll look like a princess."

"In a very short gown." Mimi put it back in the bag, her nerves anxious at the thought of wearing something that see-through for Mason. "Delilah is so good to me."

"To all of us," Valentine agreed. "No cookies for you, though."

Mimi nodded, and smiled at her daughter. Nanette

had a light dusting of crumbs on her lips. It made Mimi happy to see her daughter so happy. She and Mason were working things out all right. Nanette didn't seem to be stressed or negatively affected by the changes in her life.

Mimi was grateful for that. There had been many times over the years that she had worried about how the truth would affect Nanette.

"She's flourishing, isn't she?" Valentine said, getting up to wrap the cookies.

"Mommy, I want a puppy," Nanette said, "with one of those pink feather collars."

Mimi looked at Valentine, her eyes wide.

"Mason told her they were for the puppies," Valentine said with a wink. "Will you be wearing something that matches pink feathers tonight?"

"I don't know," Mimi hedged. "Probably not."

"Go on, Mimi. Surprise him."

Mimi looked at her friend, tantalized, she had to admit, by the thought of being daring. "We've never had a date," she murmured.

"There's always a first."

Nanette munched a cookie and played with some sprinkles in a shaker can on the table.

"Do you love him, Mimi?" Valentine asked softly, walking to the sink to wash out a pan.

"I do," Mimi said. "I always have." She thought about what was bothering her—her inner tuning fork was vibrating like mad with anxiety. "While I'm all for being sexy and fun, our relationship *is* based on sex. Shouldn't there be something else?" Mimi asked softly, following Valentine to the sink to help her wash pans—and to keep Nanette's ears safe.

"Friendship is good," Valentine said. "You have that with Mason."

Mimi shook her head. "We did. It isn't like it was, though."

"Maybe because it's maturing."

"I don't know." Valentine had a point. Mason had changed. She had, too. "Maturing would make sense, though."

"Right. Like a favorite dress. One day, it doesn't fit the same. It's still a pretty dress, but your body has matured. Changed. Gotten better."

Mimi laughed. "Okay."

"So, pink feathers figure into your plans tonight?"

Mimi wiped the crumbs off Nanette's chin with a smile, and kissed the tip of her daughter's nose. "Maybe."

TWO HOURS LATER, after Mimi had left Nanette with Valentine for babysitting, she stood in front of the long mirror in her room and took a deep breath. Then she slid the gown that Delilah had given her over her head.

It was lovely, even if it was very revealing. In fact, it revealed all the right things in an innocent, yet devilish manner, the twinkles casting light over the curves of her body. Mimi shivered, thinking about how Mason had made love to her.

Tonight was not the night for this, she decided, feeling too chicken to proceed. "Nor these," she said, picking up the feather handcuffs with a perplexed look.

Banging on her door pulled a shriek from her. Instinctively, she threw her bed blanket over herself. "Who is it?"

"Mason."

She blinked. "You're early!"

"My watch says seven. If you're not ready, I can come on in, anyway."

"No, thanks," Mimi said. She looked at her bedside table, realizing the clock was blinking. "We must have had a power surge, because my clock isn't right."

"All those blow-dryers," Mason said. "Must have been a busy day in the salon."

"Hang on a sec." She dropped the handcuffs on the bed and looked around for something to cover herself with. "Mason, you could go sit in the sunroom."

"You know, I've been having this fantasy—"

Mimi wrapped a sheet around her and jerked the door open. "Not out in the hall you don't, with everybody's ears pressed to the doors. Come in, sit down and behave."

"Wow," he said, "you look great. Toga, toga."

She gave him a discouraging eyebrow raise.

Laughing, he sat down on her bed, leaning back comfortably. "Hey, what are these?" Holding up the handcuffs, he said, "Oh, that's right. Puppy collars. Speaking of fantasies…it seems yours are going pretty well."

Irked, she said, "The handcuffs aren't mine."

"Since I'm the sheriff, I could put them on you. If you'd like."

"No, Mason. I wouldn't like." She turned away, not willing to laugh at his teasing expression. Instantly, she felt a tiny tug on the blanket she wore.

"What's under here?" Mason asked.

She snatched the material from his fingers. "I was trying to get dressed."

"So you're naked?" He leaned back on the bed, folding his arms behind his head with a smile. "I have fond memories of that."

"I'm not naked," Mimi snapped.

"Then you don't need this," Mason said, leaning

up and tugging the blanket harder than he had before. It slipped from her fingers and landed on the floor. "Wow. Is that for me?" he asked, seemingly amazed by the sheer confection he'd unveiled. "Because if it is, *thank you.*"

His gaze made a fast journey from her breasts to her toes, then back up for a more leisurely, concentrated perusal. She snatched the blanket off the floor, glaring at him. "No, it's not for you."

"I'll try to earn it sometime, then," Mason said. "Wow, Mimi. You're *hot.* I've had pinup calendars that weren't as sexy as you."

"It isn't anything you haven't seen before," she said, cross and embarrassed, as she pulled the blanket to her chest.

"Yeah, it is. Nipples, for one thing." He leaned back on the bed again, but his gaze stayed on her. "And the rest goes unmentioned, although not forgotten, now that I've seen it. You are a *true* blonde, Mimi Cannady."

Mimi stared at him. "You helped deliver my baby, Mason."

"Yeah, but I wasn't focusing on your, you know, personal assets," he said with a grin. "There was a sheet, and it wasn't all that bright. I was in a hurry and nervous. All I remember is a wee little girl sliding into my hands, much less attractive than a birthed heifer and yet far louder than anything I'd ever heard before."

"Mason! How can you say that about your daughter?" Mimi asked, trying not to laugh. "She was a beautiful baby."

"And the other times that I could have seen you," Mason said thoughtfully, "once was at night in our field, which I enjoyed, but obviously didn't give me a great view, and then the other day... Mimi, I don't know what got into me. I should apologize except I enjoyed it so much. Still didn't get to see your nipples, though."

"Well, now you have," she said, feeling her nipples tighten. "Could you leave while I finish dressing?"

"Not until you answer my question. Since you've always slept in big, ugly T-shirts, as long as I've ever known you, what's made you suddenly change into a hot mama?"

She raised her chin. "It was a gift from Delilah, if you must know."

"Ah." Mason rose. "Should have expected the hand of experience on that purchase."

"What does that mean?" Mimi demanded.

"Just that Delilah knows what a man likes." He grinned. "Mimi, I'm going. We'll do this date another time."

Mimi was stunned. "Why?"

"Because we're going to make love if I stay, and that's not what tonight was supposed to be about."

Mimi looked at him. "Mason, I believe you're scared," she said and dropped the blanket.

Raw desire raked his features. He hesitated only for a split second before grabbing her and pulling her onto the bed with him. The handcuffs fell on the floor, but Mimi told herself there would be plenty of time for those later.

AN HOUR LATER, Mimi awakened, still glowing from the lovemaking she and Mason had shared. He had one arm over her, and a great hairy leg wrapped around hers. It felt wonderful.

It felt permanent.

She tapped Mason on the shoulder. "Hey."

He raised his head and grinned at her. "Hey, Noisy."

"I am not!"

Sitting up, he ran a hand through his dark hair. "Let's just say I think all the ladies decided to have dinner out to avoid the symphony."

He was exaggerating, as usual. Mimi sat up, keeping the sheet tucked primly under her armpits. "Do you know that we never use a condom?"

"Why should we?" Mason demanded. "We want more children."

Putting on his jeans, he stood tall as he zipped them. Mimi admired his bare chest and his strong posture for a moment before he surprised her by saying, "You're coming back to the ranch with me right now. Being here serves no purpose." He scratched his head. "Pack your suitcase. Keep the gown. It works for me." He tossed her small travel bag on the bed and began cleaning out the dresser drawers.

"And then what?" Mimi asked, watching him busily run her life, which was a strange thing considering that all these years, she'd run his.

"Then we get married," Mason said. "I don't think you know how to date worth a damn. And in spite of my best intentions, I don't seem to be able to stay away from you, Mimi Cannady."

Chapter Thirteen

Once Mason said he wasn't any good at proper courtship, he felt a load lift from his shoulders. Why
should he feel bad about it? He and Mimi belonged
together. They always had; this component of their
relationship was just different.

He watched her with a mixture of lust and
powerful attraction as she put on her clothes. Affection. Man, she had him in a stew.

She always had.

"Let's go get you a ring and do this right,"
Mason said.

"All right," Mimi said, shocking him with her ac-
quiescence.

He gave her a suspicious eyeing. "No argument?"

"No." She shrugged a bare shoulder, and Mason
nearly tossed her back into the bed. But she shook her

head at him. "Uh-uh, you're getting that look in your eyes again, and I have to wash the sheets before I leave."

"Let me help you strip the bed," Mason said. "I taught my brothers how to change beds. I can do this in four minutes flat and you'll never see a wrinkle."

"Really?" Mimi folded the blankets while Mason dismantled the pretty bedding. "I always admired the fact that you made the boys keep a clean house. You would have thought a bunch of guys living in a fraternity-like atmosphere would have had cleanliness issues. But you never did."

"I allowed the occasional boot heel on the coffee table, which Helga does not. But," he said, remembering the dark days of old times, "I'm sure child protective services would have been breathing down my neck if we hadn't been clean. And I was determined to keep us all together." Straightening, he looked at her. "I don't give up anything that is mine, Mimi Cannady. Think about that before you head down to the jewelers with me."

She raised her head, giving him the blunt side of a saucy chin and snapping blue eyes, an expression he'd seen many times and which never failed to amuse him. "Is that your declaration of love?"

He took the fresh sheets she handed him. "I made

that already, when I made love to you. You can call my last statement a promise of commitment."

She laughed and finished dressing. "So what about your father's journal?" Mimi asked.

The smile slid from his face. "What about it?"

"When are you going to read it?"

"I don't know." Frowning, he wondered the same thing. "When we all agree to."

"Before or after we get engaged?"

"What does the journal have to do with us?"

"Because with my luck, you'll find something in there that makes you go off in a completely different direction. One time, you disappeared for months, in case you don't recall," Mimi said.

His frown deepened. "I would never leave you and Nanette."

She nodded. "I just wonder if it wouldn't be best to put the past behind you before you take a big step like marriage." With one hand, she reached out and touched him, and the real thing he was running from came rushing back to him with a fierce blast. "You've spent a lot of years hurting from your father's abandonment, Mason. That kind of thing isn't easy for anyone to deal with," she said softly. "I know. So let's not rush this…because that's how it feels. Sort of…rushed."

He looked at her, realizing that, once again, she

had guessed his fears. She knew him better than anyone on the planet. Compartmentalizing had been his thing for years: keeping order and strict discipline, for himself and his brothers. Having everything his way had been his refuge against pain.

"I can't promise you when we'll read it," he said.

"I know." Her hand slipped away from his arm, but she smiled. "You'll feel better once you do. And so will I. Propose to me then."

It sounded good, but still, he was reluctant. "You and I could get married, then maybe when I face the past, I'll sit down and have a good cry on your shoulder," he said.

"I'll be around for you to cry on."

"Around?"

"At my dad's. You're just going to have to share Nanette without being a horse's ass."

"So we'll really date."

"Just like we never did," she said with a soft smile.

"I'm still sleeping with you at night. My family's not going to be away from me."

Mimi laughed. "Dad would gladly give you a room in the house. But you have to knock on the front door."

"I know. He told me," Mason said. "The badge calls."

"Right. You signed on for it. Respect is your calling now."

"Will you put that gown away until we work this out?"

"Yes," Mimi said. "And I'll buy you a pair of black silk boxers for the big night."

He raised an eyebrow. "Black silk boxers? Don't think I can sit in a saddle in those."

She smiled and clicked her suitcase closed. "There won't be a horse in the room, so it won't matter."

"Yeah," Mason said, starting to feel better, "there'll be a lady. Don't forget these," he said, putting the pink feather handcuffs into her suitcase. "Now that I know what you've been hiding, I want to make certain I make all your bad-girl fantasies come true one day."

He couldn't wait for that day. But Mimi was right. It was time to say goodbye to the past.

A WEEK LATER, MASON LAID his father's journal on the table in the center of the room. He looked around at all his brothers. The wives were in town at the Union Junction Salon, having a tea for Mimi, as they'd decided that Mason and Mimi's agreement was somewhat less official than an engagement, but more permanent than what it had been before. With all the wives in town, and the children, the ladies had decided now was as good a time as any to celebrate an engagement, even an unofficial one.

It was time for the annual Fourth of July family gathering, and Mason had decided this was the right time to talk to his brothers. Last had been right; it was better to do this as a family.

"I want to talk to you," he told his brothers. "Hawk and Jellyfish found a journal of Dad's." Just saying that made a circle of dread sink into his stomach. "This is it," he said, pointing to it, "and it's up to you what we do with it."

Silence met that statement. Mason looked around the room, realizing they were looking to him for leadership.

"I have to admit to some ambivalence. I'm glad that he was healthy enough to keep a journal. I'll also admit to some…anger that he left." Mason rubbed his chin, trying to keep the dam in place before a wall of emotions burst through. "Maybe the answers we always wanted are in there. And maybe it'll just give us a lot more questions." He hesitated before taking a deep breath. "We've all been through a lot, and we're all happy now. We got through the bad years. We didn't get separated. It made us tougher, stronger, I guess, and it made us compassionate."

More silence. Mason scratched at his beard, which

he'd been growing for the past week in a moody gesture of defiance. Mimi hadn't minded the growth, which was a good thing, since he slept with her every night. Oh, he knew he wasn't supposed to, but he wasn't about to go without his girl. He'd made a lot of concessions, but that one he wasn't going to give. Every night, he knocked on the sheriff's door. The sheriff let him in like a long-lost son, and Mason went up and read his daughter a bedtime story, kissing her good-night as if his life depended upon it, which it did.

Then he slept in the guest room. In the night, as if in a sleepwalker's trance, he got in bed with Mimi. He never made love to her, but he did snuggle against her back, holding her to him.

Those were the only hours of peace he'd known recently. Nothing was expected of him, and all he did was bask in the gentle oasis that was Mimi. He was out of the house before anyone awakened. His heart, of course, stayed behind.

Fannin raised a palm. "I don't see the point of opening a can of worms, Mason."

Bandera nodded. "Maybe the right thing to do is just be glad Dad was in good condition. I don't see the point in reading words that weren't meant for us."

"How do we know they weren't?" Last asked.

"Because he never even sent us a letter," Tex said.

"It can't matter after all these years," Laredo pointed out. "I'd like to know what he wrote."

"I'd like to know," Ranger agreed, "but I'm hesitant, too. What good does it serve? If we hadn't found the journal, we wouldn't have read it, so maybe we shouldn't read it now."

"You act like there's something bad in there," Navarro said. "Dad probably wrote happy things."

"He was upset enough to leave his family," Bandera said. "Why in the hell would you think it's a happy journal? How many men do you know who keep journals when they're happy?"

"Easy, boys," Calhoun said. "Let's keep this cool."

Frisco Joe stood. "I vote we table it for now. Until Christmas, when we have our next family gathering. That would give us plenty of time to think about it and decide if any or all of us want to know."

"Good idea," Crockett said. "What do you think, Mason?"

Mason frowned. He wasn't certain Mimi would marry him under those terms. Yet the idea made complete sense. Every brother had to decide if he wanted to know what was between those pages, because it would affect each of them in some way or another. No matter what, good or bad, it would change all of them. "All right," he said. "Christmas Eve, before mass, we meet back here."

"No," Last said, and it was just like old times as everyone leaned forward to hear what the family philosophe had to say. "Not Christmas Eve and not Christmas. We don't take those times away from our families. The day after Christmas, while the ladies and kids are hitting the day-after sales in the malls."

That pleased everyone in the room, so they all jumped on the baby brother and pounded him a little for the sake of nostalgia. Mason picked up the journal, slid it into a drawer for safekeeping and quietly left.

He had another family to think about: *his* family.

MASON HEADED TOWARD Mimi's town house, looking forward to what had become his evening routine. He wanted to tell her that the past had been dealt with, in as satisfactory a manner as he could manage it. A decision had been turned over to his brothers, and as far as he was concerned, he was leaving the past behind.

His mind was celebrating this fact when he saw a strange couple of men walking through the center of town, in front of the salon. Frowning, Mason decided to see what they were up to. It was, after all, his town to protect now.

Parking his truck, he followed on foot. They had disappeared around the back of the salon. Even more concerned, Mason felt for his weapon and his handcuffs. Having both, he confidently headed into the darkened shadows.

When the board hit him across the face, knocking him to his knees, the last thing that came to Mason's mind as he lay in the gravel outside was that Mimi hadn't hurt him; it was his own overconfidence that had finally knocked him to his knees.

Chapter Fourteen

"Where's Mason?" Sheriff Cannady asked his daughter when she finished putting Nanette to bed.

Mimi closed the door to Nanette's room. "I don't know. Why?"

The sheriff looked at his watch. "He's usually here by now."

Mimi laughed. "You do like your schedules set and kept."

He nodded. "Yes, I do. Consistency is good for a family. Mason gets here. I let him in. I drink my glass of warm milk, and I go to bed. Nanette gets a kiss from her father good-night, and in the morning, when I hear the front door close, I know it's time to get up and get my newspaper."

"Dad, I love you," Mimi said.

He nodded. "I know. Think you should call him."

"He's a big boy. He can take care of himself. Come into the kitchen and I'll warm you that milk." Secretly, she didn't want to think about the fact that maybe Mason wasn't coming.

"Wouldn't be like him not to call," the sheriff said gruffly.

"He has all his family in town. I'm sure they're keeping him busy," Mimi said, remembering the days when she'd desperately wanted to be included as part of the Jefferson family. To a young girl with no siblings, twelve rowdy brothers had made her wistful.

"Call his cell," her dad said.

"Dad, he'll get here if he gets here, and if not, there's a reason." Mimi didn't want her father to know that she was beginning to wonder herself. "You're making me worry."

"No point in worrying if you call him."

"All right." It wasn't like Mason not to call and let her know exactly what was going on. All their lives, one thing Mason had always been was reliable. She waited impatiently as his cell rang and then kicked over to his recorded message. With a shrug, she hung up the phone. "Guess he's busy."

Her father nodded. "Think I'll take a drive."

"Oh, no, you don't. Not without me," Mimi said,

knowing her father's old instincts were rousing. "You shouldn't be out late."

"You can't leave your child, Mimi," her father pointed out reasonably, "and I'll be fine. It's just a drive in the nice evening breeze."

"No, it's not," Mimi said, getting her car keys. "I know exactly what you're doing, and if someone's going to check on Mason, it needs to be me."

"Call me if you need me. I can call Barley to come sit with Nanette. Or one of the stylists. Or Crockett and Valentine since they're so close. Crockett's probably up painting, anyway."

"You get your milk and get back on schedule," Mimi said. "I'll report in when I return."

It was past eleven. She didn't expect to find Mason; she felt certain he'd fallen asleep at his house. With all his family at home, he and his brothers might even be up late talking.

She was very surprised when she turned into the town square and saw Mason's truck parked outside the salon. Two men stood near his truck, looking very much as though they were talking to Mason.

Only she didn't see Mason in the truck. Mimi shut off her truck, looped her purse over her shoulder, got out and quietly closed her door. Pulling out a cell phone, she rang her house and quietly said, "I'm on the square. Send help."

Then she decided to play dumb. Maybe they weren't really breaking into Mason's truck. They could be peering at it because it was a fine example of a rolling steel castle, but the way they kept glancing around made her think they were nervous.

"Excuse me," she said.

They whirled to look at her. "Well, now," one of them said.

"The welcome committee," the other said with a sneer.

That didn't sound promising. "The man who owns that truck will get real twitchy if there's even a fingerprint on it. You might want to find something else to look at."

"Like you?" The shorter of the two walked toward her.

"Did you happen to see him?" Mimi asked. "The man who drives this truck?"

"Think he's sleeping right now, sugar," the taller one said, approaching as well.

Not liking how close they were getting, she pulled her hair-spray can from her purse and she gave them both a righteous spraying in their faces, then ran toward the Union Junction Salon.

She didn't make it to the porch before the ladies came spilling out the door. Lights went on all over the house, and Mimi could see her friends were armed with skillets and pans and a broomstick or two.

Mimi decided to let the girls do their thing alone once she spied a cowboy hat lying in the street to the side of the big house. Running over to the hat, she found Mason trying to get up and not having a lot of success.

"Mason!" She put an arm under him and helped him to his feet. "What happened?"

"Think I took a two-by-four in the face," Mason said. "Sheriffing's not going to be pretty for my complexion."

"This is all my fault. I shouldn't have talked you into running for the office—" She blinked, and then tugged at him impatiently. "I think you have a concussion."

"No, I don't." He squinted across the street where a policeman was loading up the two thugs the Union Junction ladies had corralled. "What are you doing out here, anyway? You should be at home with Nanette."

"You should, too," Mimi said crossly. "My father sent me to look for you."

He looked down at her. Mimi winced. She was

pretty sure his nose was broken, and there was a gap over his eyebrow that was going to require a stitch or two. "Fortunately for you, Doc Gonzalez doesn't live too far away."

A throng of women encircled them, with cries of "Poor Mason," and "You should have hit them harder with that skillet, Marni!" and Mason lapped it all up like a conquering hero come home from war. They tried to usher him and Mimi into their home, but Mason shook his head.

"Thanks, ladies. And thanks for backing up my girl. Union Junction's safe with so many hot lady deputies. But my two girls need me at home."

Mimi was strangely glad to hear such a possessive tone in Mason's voice.

"You're going straight to Doc's," she said.

"After that, your house?"

"Maybe." She smiled. "I have something to tell you," she said, as they walked toward his truck together.

"I have something to tell you, too, but I think I'll wait for my anesthetic before I have my say. You go ahead."

Mimi helped him into the seat. "Everything can wait until later."

"This can't," he said. "My brothers voted not to read the journal until the day after Christmas. Gives us something to do while you ladies are out spending our money."

"Put a lid on your male chauvinistic side," Mimi said, secretly relieved that Mason was in good enough shape to be thinking about their relationship. "I don't need your money, Mason Jefferson." She went around and got inside the driver's side. "I do want your keys."

He sighed. "Be careful with my truck," he said, handing them to her.

"More careful than you were with your face. Nanette's going to cry when she sees you."

"Yeah. I'll tell her…some good fairy tale. So, does it bother you that we're tabling all discussion about the journal until December?"

"No," Mimi said, "what matters is that you acknowledged it, brought it out in the open and gave everyone a choice in the matter, instead of hiding from it."

"I don't hide from anything," Mason said with a growl, but she laughed at him.

"I'm relieved, Mason. I'm glad everyone is satisfied."

"Tell me what you have to say now."

It wasn't the time she would have chosen to tell him, but at least it would keep his mind off any pain he was feeling, and conversation kept her nerves from shredding. "We're not pregnant."

He straightened. "Were we trying?"

"We weren't not trying," Mimi said, cross again. "We didn't use precautions."

"Oh." Mason smiled at her, a slow, lazy smile in the darkness as they pulled up to Doc's. "That means we get to practice a lot more."

Mimi shook her head. "How can you think about sex with your face all banged up?"

He helped himself from the truck. "Because I know that when Doc gets me bandaged up, I'm going to be sleeping at Mimi's house. And that makes me think about sex."

Mimi wasn't thinking about sex. In fact, she was going to put Mason to bed and tell him not to even so much as roll over! He'd frightened her, more than she cared to admit. It had been all she could do to act like a sheriff's daughter and not scream when she saw him lying on the ground.

Cool, calm, collected.

She was barely holding herself together.

As MIMI DROVE, Mason decided his face hurt like hell and his pride was pretty damaged, too. How could he have let those two-bit hoods jump him? He should have learned something in police training, but clearly, he hadn't been thinking about two-by-fours. Wanting more experience, he had gone into the city and taken some squad car rides and some courses that were beneficial to being a sheriff. And then got laid low by petty creeps. He was lucky he had all his teeth.

He was also lucky that Mimi wasn't the squeamish type. His shirt was pretty red with blood, though one of the ladies had handed him a cloth to press against his wound.

She banged on Doc's door. "Hang on and let's see what Doc has to say."

"But then I want to talk seriously to you, Mimi," Mason said, trying to make his voice stern and failing miserably. Doc let them in, sending Mason right to a couch so he could look at him under the light of his reading lamp.

"You really need to take a run down to the hospital," Doc said.

"I don't wanna." Mason closed his eyes, feeling very tired all of a sudden. "You've stitched us Jeffersons under more exciting circumstances."

Doc sighed. "All right. Thing is, I think you should be scanned for a concussion."

"What good would it do?" Mason asked, hearing Mimi groan. "I'm not trying to be stubborn. If I have a concussion, it's not like there's anything they can do about it. I'll just rest at home."

"I know you won't rest," Doc said.

"I'll make him rest," Mimi said, and Mason perked right up.

"I can stay at your house and let you be my nurse?"

"Hold still," Doc said. "Unless you'd prefer I sew up your lips instead of this gash."

Mason sighed. He felt Mimi move restlessly beside him and wondered if she was getting light-headed from seeing blood and stitches. Actually, he was starting to get light-headed himself. "Make me look good for my girls, Doc," he said.

"Is he all right?" Mimi asked.

"Yeah," Doc said, snipping a stitch off. "He's an ornery ol' rascal, but he'll be fine. Some love and attention ought to be as good on his soul as a stay in the hospital. And I'm pretty certain he prefers you and Nanette to any nurse they have over there, although they're all very competent."

Mimi looked at Mason's poor bleeding face and swollen mouth. A shiver ran over her. What if her dad hadn't sent her out? What if those thugs had done worse?

"Mason," she said, when Doc went to get some antiseptic. "Mason, I'll marry you now."

His hand shot out and grabbed hers. "The Curse of the Broken Body Parts strikes again. I'll hold you to that promise, after I date you for a suitable amount of time, of course, so you will have something to look back on fondly."

Mimi jerked her hand back, surprised. "I thought you didn't believe in the Curse."

"I didn't. Now I do." He gave her a gimlet eye. "Since it's happened, I'm going with it. When are you marrying me?"

Mimi blinked. "You'll need some time to recover—"

"No. I won't. I'm tough. And you're not getting any younger, so we better start working on that family."

"Mason!" Mimi glanced at Doc, slightly annoyed by the teasing.

"In that little toy box the Union Junction girls have, can they dig out a nurse's uniform? I'd really like to see you in one of those. It's always been a—"

"Mason," Mimi said, "you may be bordering on delirium. Please go back to sleep."

"Think I will."

Doc laughed. "Who would have thought Mason Jefferson had such a wild—oh. Sorry, Mimi," Doc said, his eyes twinkling. "My patients usually aren't so loquacious."

"Mason's been surprising me these days, too." Mimi wondered if Mason would remember her offer to marry him. He was being such a rascal she wasn't sure if she wanted him to remember!

"You're just the right medicine for him, Mimi. There, all done."

He put away his equipment, and Mimi looked at Mason with some puzzlement. "Mason, Doc says you're fine to go home."

"Good." Mason slowly moved his legs over the side of the sofa and stood, letting Mimi support him. "I feel just a wee bit woozy, like I've had one too many beers."

"Do you want me to drive you out to the ranch? Your family is all there, and I know you don't want to miss seeing them."

"Nope. I want peace and quiet and I won't get it there. Your bed is fine."

Mimi blushed as she saw a tiny smile flit across Doc's face. "Thank you, Doc, for seeing us at this hour."

"You just keep that reprobate still, Mimi. It's going to take your finest nursing skills to keep him in his place."

"Good night, Doc." She helped Mason toward his truck, glad when he regained his own firm footing. After they got in, she drove toward her town house. "What are we going to tell Nanette?"

"That things happen for a reason, and Mommy should have married me in the first place."

Mimi frowned. "That's not what I meant, nor is it true."

"But now that you've hurt me, I think it's a sign we should get on with the show."

"Mason, I did not hurt you," Mimi said hotly. "You walked into someone's two-by-four. I wasn't even around!"

"I'm falling in love with you," Mason said. "It's the Curse."

"Oh, goodness," Mimi said. "I can't tell if you're being weird because you are or because of the shots Doc gave you."

"Mimi," Mason said, his voice serious suddenly, "I have a bone to pick with you."

"You always do. Pick away."

"What were you thinking going up to those thugs and chatting with them like you were Miss Union Junction?"

"I was looking for you."

"Don't do that again," Mason said. "Only one of us is sheriff, and *I* wear the badge."

Chapter Fifteen

Mason saw Mimi's back go tight and knew she was about to let him have it. She'd yowl about him being a chauvinist, and that would be good, because it would keep his mind off the pain.

Not the pain in his face, which hurt, but the pain of seeing his girl get snippy with two no-goods. For the first time in his life, he'd been frozen, unable to do anything, his body pretty much defying even the will to stand up.

Later, when he was more rational, he would make sure she'd never do that again. Right now, it was enough to give her a small tongue-lashing. Closing his eyes, he listened to her heap abuse on him for his smart remark.

What had he gotten himself into? Mimi was always going to be a sheriff's daughter. She would never think anything of going right at any problem, and since she'd thought Mason needed saving, there she'd gone.

His lips pursed. "I do not want you saving me ever again, Mimi Cannady."

She gasped. "That's a strange thank-you."

"From now on, I want you to stay home with Nanette." There at least he would know she was safe, with their daughter, and not into mischief. "If you think there's a problem, you can send my brothers."

But next time there won't be a problem because I won't have my mind so wrapped up in Miss Independence.

As soon as he thought that, he realized he was kidding himself. If he married her—*when* he married her—she was going to keep his brain running in dizzy circles. It was who Mimi was and why he couldn't get enough of her, but God, she made him kooky.

"You know, your dad would have wanted your mother to stay home," he began, and as soon as he said that, he knew he'd struck a wound far deeper than the ones he'd just suffered.

Silence met his words.

Mason winced, kicking himself. "Mimi, I'm sorry. I…wasn't thinking about what I was saying, I swear."

She didn't say anything. Once she stopped the

truck at her town house, she got out, made sure he could stand upright, then opened the front door.

Sheriff Cannady cursed when he saw Mason's face. "Looks like you got the wrong end of a baseball bat, son, not that there's a right end."

"Something like that," Mason said, desperately needing a bed and wishing the pain meds would wear off so he could think more clearly.

"Mason, I'm making up the guest bedroom for you," Mimi said, her tone stony. "And remember, Doc doesn't want you moving for forty-eight hours because of your concussion."

"Concussion?" Mimi's dad asked. "You're going to have a hell of a headache most likely. For a few days at least."

"I already do," Mason said, treading up the stairs. He had a helluva heartache, too, but he didn't know if forty-eight hours of rest was the proper course of action for that or not.

"HE'S SO PIGHEADED, Dad," Mimi said, putting away the cups after she and her father had late-night tea. Tea never kept her awake, but tonight she'd probably stay awake, caffeine or not. "He was upset with me for going after him."

"Well," her father said, "that's probably my fault.

I felt it was best for you to go, since I didn't feel anything was really wrong—I just wanted to ease my worries. I didn't want to look like ol' nosy Pop going to check up on his daughter's beau."

Mimi smiled. "I don't think Mason would have thought that, but at the same time, I was worried, too. I wanted to know where he was." But Mason wasn't going to see it any way but his, of course.

That was something she needed to accept about loving him the way she did: he was contrary, and he wanted everything to fit his views. "Unfortunately," she told her dad, "he heard me confront the bad guys. It's really set him off."

Her father nodded. "Think maybe you shouldn't have."

"I was…worried. They didn't look like they were up to any good. Still, I couldn't be certain. We don't usually have anything but the odd mischief-maker come through Union Junction."

"Mimi, my girl, you know it didn't make two bits of difference once you got it in your head to take matters into your own hands. If Mason's gonna be the sheriff, you're gonna have to let him be a man, honey."

Mimi blinked. "Ugh, I don't like anything about the sound of that."

Her father laughed. "I imagine you don't."

"Maybe he'll forget."

"I don't know." Her father snapped a cookie in half. "The thing about the male of the species is that he's very possessive about what belongs to him. No man wants his woman to be in danger."

"Belongs to him? Woman? Dad, I don't think I've ever heard you talk like this," Mimi said with a teasing smile.

He shrugged. "It's hard to remember the feeling, but I know I had it once."

"Oh, Dad." Mimi's smile faded.

"I made my peace with things over the years. I have to be honest, though, I admire Mason's determination to make certain his family stays together. It takes two to feel that way, you know. Commitment." He sighed. "Not so many people understand that word anymore."

"Maybe what I think is stubbornness on Mason's part is really commitment," Mimi murmured.

Her dad stood. "Well, I enjoyed the tea and cookies, daughter." Leaning down, he kissed her forehead. "You're a good girl, Mimi. You'll make the right decisions for everyone concerned."

"I love you, Daddy. Good night."

Mimi watched her father head up the stairs. For the

first time, she felt some comfort about the situation with Mason. She'd been the driver in their relationship for so long that she hadn't given him much credit for *his* driving skills—nor a chance to assert them.

When the revelation came, it left Mimi breathless. She had always wanted control because she was afraid. Abandonment by her mother had made her want to take care of everything in her environment. Rescue it. Make it happy. Whatever *it* was—fill in the blank—she took charge.

And because of his father, Mason was the same.

"Which means we're going to butt heads every day of our lives, just like he did with his brothers," Mimi murmured. Neither of them trusted enough to let go and relax.

Her father was right, even if he'd couched it in unpalatable terms. If she loved Mason, if she wanted to spend her life with him, she had to realize that just as she'd sent him off to read his father's journal, in case there was some hidden booby trap that would affect their relationship, *she* needed to be doing some housekeeping in her own life.

She felt as though a boulder had lifted off her spirit.

It was okay to be fragile. Okay to be weepy, scared and cranky. It was even okay to allow Mason to make some decisions. He could be the leader sometimes, and she could follow. In an adult relationship there was give and take, compromise. It didn't matter who the leader was. As long as their hearts cared more about togetherness.

MASON AWAKENED to find a fully dressed Mimi tucked next to him, burrowed against his back. He started to grin, then realized that hurt. But the smile was inside him.

His smile grew steadier when he realized that what had awakened him was a sweet little angel staring down at him. "What is it, honey?" he asked Nanette. "Can't you sleep?"

"You didn't read me a bedtime story," she whispered, so she wouldn't awaken her mother.

"I was on my way here," he said, tucking her into bed next to him, right up under his chin. With Mimi's arm over his waist and his daughter's sweet-smelling hair under his chin, surely he was the happiest man on earth. "I'll read you two tomorrow night. You go to sleep now."

"'Kay."

He kissed the top of her head, allowing his eyes to drift shut again.

"Why is Mommy sleeping in here?"

"Because I bumped my head and the doctor said

I have a bad headache. So she's keeping an eye on me, like she does for you when you're sick."

"Oh," Nanette said. "How did you bump your head?"

"I wasn't paying attention," he said with a sigh. "But I'm not going to do that anymore."

Nanette giggled. "You might."

"I don't think so. It hurt."

Mostly what had hurt was watching Mimi bossing around a couple of bad guys.

"I love you, Daddy," Nanette said, her voice already sounding sleepy again.

"I love you, too, sweetie," he said, his own eyes closing.

He was very grateful Mimi had made him a father, and that alone was enough to make him forgive her just about anything.

MANY HOURS LATER, when the sunlight was streaming into the room, he felt Mimi try to pull away and leave the bed. He held her arm tight so she couldn't. Rolling over to face her, he said, "Good morning," and kissed her forehead.

"Good morning. You're uglier than last night," Mimi said, gently touching his forehead. "Can I get you anything?"

"No. Just you." He pulled her tightly against him.

She giggled. "Mason, why is Nanette sleeping in here?"

"She wondered the same thing about you."

"And what did you tell her?"

"That this was the most comfy bed in the house, and, so, just like in *Goldilocks and the Three Bears,* everyone wants in it. Mommy Bear, Papa Bear and Baby Bear."

Mimi smiled. "That's not the way the story went, and I doubt you said any of that because I would have heard the two of you jabbering."

"And yet you didn't." He kissed the tip of her nose. "You snore like a hardworking ditchdigger, lady."

"I do not!"

He kissed her lips. "Yeah, you do. It's all the stress from crime fighting."

"That's not funny."

"No, it's not," Mason said, giving her fanny a tiny slap. "No more badass chick adventures for you."

"I'm going to let you be the big man from now on," Mimi said primly.

He let out a roar. "What a sweet little thing you are in the morning. So accommodating! But I think your nose is growing, Mimi Cannady."

"No. I mean it. I realized last night that what I did was dumb. Brave, maybe, but also dumb."

He chuckled. "You are brave. You also want to be right in the thick of everything that's happening in life and with everybody's business."

She gave him a pretend tweak on the abdomen. "For a guy with a concussion, you sure do think you know a lot. Maybe you should rest your brain."

"There's my saucy wench." He nipped her shoulder.

"Mason," Mimi said, running a finger down his chest, "I had this bright idea that you would make a great sheriff. You know? But you're not really cut out for this job. I want you to let Shoeshine Johnson take over the job."

"Shoeshine can't," Mason said. "He runs the school bus, and his own farm."

"We could run the school bus," Mimi said.

"We could," Mason said, "but I like my bright, shiny badge."

She smiled wistfully. "It looks good on you. I just don't want you to wear it anymore."

"Has someone gotten cold feet?" He raised her chin and looked in her eyes. "You're the one who got me into this gig."

"I know. You made that clear last night when you said it was my fault you'd gotten hurt."

Mason forced himself not to grin so he wouldn't pop a stitch, but he thought Mimi's little fit of conscience was adorable. "You've never taken me seriously before."

"That's because you've never been injured like that before. They could have killed you, or paralyzed you, or—"

Mason stopped her talking by kissing her. When he estimated he'd enjoyed about thirty seconds of silence, he said, "See? I'm just as good as always."

"No, you're not. Your face is purple in spots and pasty in others. Actually, it's fairly Frankensteinish, with that zigzag of stitches. What did Nanette say about your beauty treatment?"

He resisted the urge to run his hands under her nightgown. After all, his daughter was in the bed, and that just wouldn't do. "She doesn't care what I look like. She's only interested in my personality, not my looks," he teased, but Mimi didn't smile. "What's wrong?" he asked.

"I'm sorry for dragging you into this dangerous profession."

"You're a pushy broad, Mimi, but I do what I want to do." He looked at her and saw worry in her blue eyes; he could feel tension in her body. "What are you afraid of?"

"Losing you," she said softly, sending a spear into his heart.

"You mean to some bad guys?"

She nodded.

"I guess there's no one hundred percent chance that might not happen," Mason said, "but I'm pretty tough, Mimi. You can't go through life being scared."

"I have," she said, "and so did you."

He pulled back to frown down at her, puzzled.

"And it's influencing our choices now," Mimi said.

"I don't get it.

"Maybe we're just reaching out to each other now," Mimi said, "because it's what we know best."

"I don't know," Mason said. "I plan on getting to know you a hell of a lot better. I didn't realize I'd never seen your bare nipples until I caught you in that lacy thing. They're cute, Mimi. Sexy and kinda sassy, like your whole personality."

"Mason!" Mimi buried her head against his chest. "I'm trying to be practical for once in my life. So would you listen?"

"I don't like what I'm hearing."

Mimi laid a fingertip over his lips. "We've waited this long. We have plenty of time to make certain we're doing everything for the right reasons." She shook her head. "I don't want to be scared anymore. Do you?"

"Listen, Mimi, fear is when your lady thinks she's a superhero and tries to open up a can o' whoopass on two fellas who outweigh her by at least fifty pounds and are carrying a large piece of wood. Hell, you *did* open up a can o' whoopass. Where'd you get pepper spray?"

"It was actually hair spray," Mimi said. "All my friends work in a salon, and they taught me everything I know about self-preservation. However, I've always carried pepper spray because my father insisted. It just wasn't needed for those weenies."

"Oh, jeez," Mason said, "I think my heart's gonna give out." He dramatically laid a hand over his chest and rolled onto his back to stare at the ceiling. "If I'd known my woman was shaking down bad guys with a can of Dippity-do, I would have lost it."

"Not Dippity-do," Mimi said, giving him a pinch. "It was Sweet and Strong. Guaranteed by the Union Junction girls to keep every single strand of hair from moving in even the strongest Texas tornado."

He rolled over and put his lips on her neck to give her nips and kisses. "You don't wear hair spray. But I like the name, Sweet and Strong. It's just like you. And you felled those buggers like they deserved. I like a woman who knows how much I love my truck."

She gave him a play slap on the back. "Get off of me, you oaf."

"Mimi," Mason said, looking down into her eyes, "don't say you're afraid of being with me anymore."

She hesitated, and in that time, it seemed his heart stopped. Forgot how to beat. Lost its rhythm.

"I can't help it," she said. "I seem to be afraid of so much right now." Her blue eyes welled with tears. "But I love you, Mason. I really do."

"That doesn't sound like I win the prize," Mason said. "It sounds like I get runner-up or something."

"Go back to sleep," Mimi said. "In a little while I'll bring you breakfast."

"A little hemlock? Perhaps a dagger?" Mason asked, trying to tease, but the words fell flat. "Mimi, I don't need a nurse. I need you to let me hold you. Of course, if you want to wear a nurse's uniform, I won't say no. I'm not picky, but—"

"Mason, go to sleep," Mimi said. "I'll see you in a while."

But she didn't. In fact, when he awakened with a splitting headache, Mimi and Nanette had gone.

Chapter Sixteen

Mason packed a bag. Hawk had called and told him Mimi and Nanette were taking a sabbatical up there on his mountain, so not to get steamed up. Mason had appreciated the call. Mimi was just feeling crowded, and she needed to clear her head. He could handle that.

Though he didn't like being left. There were moments when the fear he'd felt as a kid, after finding his father's goodbye letter, returned to gnaw on him. Mimi hadn't left a note, but she'd just run to a friend's. She hadn't run far, and that was a good sign.

Hell, everybody had a little run in them at some time or another. Even he'd left the ranch for a while not long ago. It wouldn't matter in the end. Those were his girls, and it was always going to be that way, because Jefferson men didn't give up on their people.

If they did, folks—especially Mimi—would have given up on him a long time ago.

He knew he'd put her through the wringer over the years. She was entitled to a little healthy doubting, especially since he really did look like Frankenstein, and she clearly was rethinking whether she wanted to be Frankenstein's bride.

On the other hand, Mimi was going to have to accept that fear did not equal inaction, at least to his way of thinking. She was going to be his bride, despite her attack of cold feet.

He knew just how to warm them.

"Where you headed?" Sheriff Cannady asked Mason on his way out.

"First, I'm going to go down and visit our incarcerated friends. Want to get out of them whether they were just in a foul mood and deciding to cause a bit of trouble, or if they were up to something more sinister. Then I ship them into the city."

"I'll go with you."

"I'd appreciate that." Mason stood. "Then I'm going to go call on your daughter. She's escaped me for the moment."

Sheriff Cannady grinned. "No one ever said this would be easy, Mason."

"No, they didn't, sir."

"And you are pretty banged up. If I was Mimi, I might be having second thoughts myself."

"Well, I'm not going to let her have them too long. I heal very quickly."

"Glad you have a plan. I'm ready to go whenever you are."

"Sheriff," Mason said suddenly.

"Yes?" The older man turned to look at him.

"I'd like to ask you for your daughter's hand in marriage, sir. I promise to take very good care of her."

The sheriff grinned. "I thought you'd never ask, son. If you can catch her, you can count on my blessings."

Mason nodded. "Thank you, sir."

"And if you can't catch her...well, Mason," Sheriff Cannady said, "you still have my blessings. You're like a son to me."

"I will marry Mimi," Mason said, knowing that if he had to go to the ends of the earth to win her he would.

SHE WAS VACATIONING—Mason refused to use the word *hiding*—in a place so remote that he would never have found it without a map. He could easily envision his brother Ranger rolling down this chasm into the Native American graveyard filled with totems and beautiful drawings as he had a few years back. Hawk kept this arid, secret place free of highway debris and vagrants. In a way, Hawk's land reminded Mason of Anasazi ruins he'd once seen in a book his father had shown him. This mountain area was deserted, mystical and filled with the fabric of ghosts from the past, which suited Hawk just fine.

On top of the tree-shrouded hill and far from the ruins, Hawk had built a house. It reminded Mason of a tree house. From inside, pretty much all that could be seen was the sky and the surrounding forest and then down into the chasm. Hawk had night-vision goggles, a telescope and fine binoculars, which kept him in tune with his surroundings.

Right now, he loaned his binoculars to Mason. "Down there," he said. "You'd think they were at the beach. Nanette is picking up rocks and old pinecones."

Mason's heart thudded with gladness when he saw his family, even through the distancing glass eyes of the binoculars.

"They keep mostly quiet and to themselves," Hawk said. "And Nanette doesn't touch anything I ask her not to."

"Do you worry about snakes? Bears?"

Hawk pulled out a long-range sniper's rifle. "No. And Mimi's packing."

The hair practically stood on end on Mason's head. "Mimi's packing? Are you crazy?"

Hawk laughed. "She's packing something called Sweet and Strong."

Mason relaxed fractionally. "I don't think hair spray is going to dissuade a snake from striking or a bear from ripping them to shreds."

Hawk nodded. "But you can't protect a person from everything. And sometimes danger is mostly in the mind, you know."

"That sounds like mumbo jumbo to me."

"Only because you're closing the door to your powers of perception. Why do you hide from what you really need to know?"

Mason stared at his friend. "I have no powers of anything. Except those I've had since I was born."

"Which are?"

"Strength. Determination. Stubbornness."

Hawk pointed down to Nanette, who was tugging at her mother's dress and showing her an arrowhead she'd found. "Strength you developed because your parents fed you well and made sure you had everything. Determination you learned because you had no one to rely on but yourself after they were gone. Stubbornness is not always a good trait, but again, it is self-developed to keep the bears of disappointment and snakes of sorrow away."

Mason frowned. "So you want me to hone some flighty part of myself?"

Hawk nodded. "Might do you good."

"All right. You sound like you want to tell me something, but you can't because Mimi doesn't want you to."

"Right," Hawk said with a grin.

"She wants me to be convinced of my feelings for her, because she thinks she's led me to want her because of Nanette. She also thinks that she may end up like her mother, if she ever allows herself to slow down and get bored for a second."

Hawk nodded.

"So what do you want me to do about it?"

Hawk looked at him.

"So what do *I* want to do about it?" Mason restated.

Hawk raised a brow.

"The antidote to boredom is action," Mason said. "Right now, we're very active in our feelings for each other. Mimi needs to test a slow phase in order to feel more secure."

Hawk smiled.

"I've never known Mimi to have a slow speed. She's always traveling fast," Mason continued.

"Change is what is required in a relationship. Mimi knows this."

"Whoa," Mason said, "are you sure we're talking about my Mimi?"

They looked down into the gully. The girls were returning, and Nanette looked delighted with her basket of trophies.

"When you looked down," Hawk said, "all you saw was danger. Ugliness. Worry. Bears and snakes. That's no way to exist. I saw beautiful trees, beautiful people and a totem collection it is my privilege to guard."

"Bull," Mason said. "That's why you have a high-powered rifle with a sniper's sight on it."

Hawk laughed. "Being careful and prepared is not the same as living with fear. If one person in a relationship is always afraid, the other person eventually has to leave."

"And Mimi's afraid of many things right now, like me being sheriff."

"Yes." Hawk frowned. "I have some special things to put on your face that will help it heal so you don't bear that scar forever."

"Any scar will be a reminder to me not to let fear rule my relationships in life," Mason said. "I probably could have used that knowledge earlier."

Hawk grinned. "Mason, you couldn't have listened. You were raising twelve boys. Parents tend to be afraid at times."

"I've been afraid ever since Dad left," Mason admitted, shocked by the knowledge spreading through his mind like mist.

"I know. So how does Mimi know you won't one day leave?"

"Because I'm not my father," Mason stated.

"Maybe you are your father. Your father became ill," Hawk said sternly. "If you can imagine raising twelve boys in a remote location with little help, you can probably envision any normal human being suffering without his chosen spirit partner."

"I meant, I would never leave any family of mine," Mason said.

"Spoken from fear of abandonment," Hawk said. "And Mimi was just as abandoned. You share the same life experience. Which means you must go slowly with each other and build bonds of trust. It can't be done just using the tools you named— strength, determination, stubbornness."

"It's all I have," Mason said.

"Consider this," Hawk said. "In life, why does the ugly, skinny boy sometimes win the most beautiful, smart girl that all the neolithic guys with money are chasing?"

Mason stared at his friend.

"Great sex," Hawk said, laughing.

"Oh. I thought you were asking me some kind of deep question," Mason said sheepishly.

"I was," Hawk said, "because first the nerd had to get there. How did he do that? He *listened* to what she needed," Hawk said, walking down the hall as Mimi and Nanette came in the front door.

Mason straightened, anticipating his first glance of Mimi. She was going to be surprised to see him. Hopefully not angry. Maybe he hadn't given her enough space.

Nanette jumped into his arms, and when Mimi looked up and saw him, she smiled. Through his fear, Mason felt incomprehensible arrows of love pierce his heart.

He was never going to get over this woman. He was his father's son.

So I'd better make damn sure I listen to what she's really saying, which isn't going to be easy because I don't like to sit still. Action keeps me from thinking.

But I can. For her.

Chapter Seventeen

Mimi was glad to see Mason. While she hadn't expected him to come, she felt better knowing that he understood that her ambivalent feelings weren't completely about him.

She loved Mason. She always had. And she would never try to keep Nanette from her father. But how to explain the feelings of fear inside her?

"I'm glad you're here, Mason."

"Me, too."

"Nanette!" Hawk called down the hall. "Do you want to go visit Uncle Jellyfish and Uncle Tex and Aunt Cissy? On the boat?"

"Can I?" Nanette asked her mother with big eyes.

"Ask your father," Mimi said.

"Have a good time," Mason said. "Take your sweater."

Nanette kissed them and ran off.

"Take your sweater?" Mimi asked.

"It can get chilly on the river at night," Mason said.

"I think you just wanted to sound fatherly." Mimi smiled at him.

"Do I win points for sounding fatherly?"

"Maybe." Mimi went out onto the porch, which wrapped around the house. Mason followed, and they sat in wooden chairs Hawk had made. "It's beautiful here."

Mason nodded.

"Thank you for not being upset with me."

Mason shrugged. "I understood."

Mimi nodded and looked away. "I know I said this before, but I really think we're rushing things."

"I agree."

Mimi turned to look at Mason. "You do?"

"Absolutely."

"Oh, good." Mimi felt so much better. "I'm not sure why we were in such a rush."

"Me, neither. Except I like being with you."

She smiled. "It's like we were trying to compress a meaningful relationship into a month, when we've lived next door to each other all our lives. There's just some things that can't be rushed."

"As much as we know about each other, our relationship wasn't romantic," Mason said.

"Exactly," she said. "There could never be anyone else I'm as close to. But I need to trust myself more. I need time to adjust."

"It's almost a good thing I got hit upside the head, because it's making us slow down," Mason said, eager to go along with the listening and empathizing scenario. "Face our fears."

She laughed. "You don't have any fears."

Sure I do. Losing you. "I'm a badass," Mason said agreeably. "But even badasses have their softer side."

"So you're fine with waiting?"

If she was talking about sex, absolutely, he could wait. It wouldn't be fun, but if it mattered that much to her, then sure. "Not a problem," he said magnanimously.

"Thank you," she said, beaming.

"You're welcome," he said, feeling like the skinny kid who'd just won the girl.

"So maybe by Christmas, we'll both feel better about everything," Mimi said with a smile. "And while I'm here, I realized I owe you a more heartfelt apology."

Trying to listen while holding back a need to grab her, Mason shrugged. "For what?"

"I should have told you sooner about Nanette. I'm sorry, Mason. It was very wrong of me." She took a deep breath. "I've always been so afraid of losing you."

"I was angry, but I'm not now," Mason said. "Although in the future, I hope we can be more open with each other."

Mimi nodded. "I'm going to try."

"I will, too." There. Had he been sensitive enough? Allowed her to speak her thoughts? Had he listened?

"I don't want to be married to a sheriff," Mimi whispered. "As odd as that sounds, I understand myself better now. All my life, I thought my father was a hero. My daddy could do anything. Now I understand that every day, he put his life on the line for other people. I'm scared."

"But you got me this job," Mason said.

"Before I knew that we might get married."

Now Mason was really confused. He tried to listen harder, as Hawk had suggested. "You would have been the sheriff if I hadn't taken the job."

"And now I see how wrong I was." Mimi nodded. "I'm not cut out to be a sheriff. I'm cut out to be a mom. A daughter."

"A wife."

"I was no good at that."

"But this time you will be, because you'll be doing it for the right reason."

Mimi looked out the window, then met his gaze. "I've always wanted to be part of your family, and part of your world. Maybe subconsciously I thought marrying you was the answer."

Mason stood very still, not liking anything he was hearing. "And now?"

"Let's just wait and see what happens."

Somewhere in the back of his mind, he heard Hawk's voice telling him to cool his jets. Let her run a little, wear herself out. Eventually, she'd come to him. But unless he waited for her to come to him, she'd keep shying away. His normal method of addressing her doubts would be to grab her, kiss her and make love to her. But then what would that change?

"Christmas it is, Mimi," Mason said softly. "Come see me when you're ready. In the meantime, I'll pick up Nanette every other day and alternate weekends with you. If you like, you can have Brian draw up papers to that effect."

Tipping his hat to her, he kissed her lightly on the lips, and then he left, walking as fast as he could. Before he changed his mind and gave in to the unwelcome fear that he'd lost Mimi forever.

Damn it, it sucked to be a sensitive male.

BY THE END OF JULY, Mimi could breathe a little easier. What had happened the night Mason was injured had scared her more than she was willing to admit, and even more than she could put into words.

But three weeks after her discussion with Mason, when she'd had time to think about things, Mimi knew she missed her cowboy more than she could ever have imagined. She was going to have to come to peace with his badge.

The thing was, after being completely against running for sheriff and only doing it to keep her from having to take over her father's job, Mason had turned out to be a damn fine sheriff. He was always at the kids' schools talking about safety. He took a lot of training courses, to be better prepared for situations he hadn't encountered before.

As for the two thugs he'd sent to jail, Mason took pity on them after a while and put them to cleaning out the jail. Then he had them polish the church pews. They had a lawyer, but Mason did, too. And it didn't take long to make sure the two petty vagrants were going to spend as much time as Mason wanted making up the damage to his face and his pride.

It was, as he told his brothers, a good learning experience for him. Getting hit with a large piece of wood taught a man to rethink what he thought he knew and not just live on confidence alone.

Mimi decided Mason wasn't the only person who should learn from life's lessons, and she took up baking with Valentine at Baked Valentines. After all, Mimi was not known for excellent cooking, and if the way to a man's heart was through his stomach, then she wanted to have plenty of yummy temptations for Mason's eating pleasure.

By September, Mimi wondered if Mason was ever going to act like an interested suitor again. He picked up Nanette on his days and his weekends. The rest of the days were filled with silence, which Mimi knew was her own fault.

By October, Mimi couldn't stand it anymore. She decided it was time for the two of them to talk. Pumpkins decorated the fields around Mason's house, and Mimi felt a twinge of regret for her stubborn ways. If she hadn't been such a frightened little rabbit, she and Mason would have put out the pumpkins for the children together.

She was determined not to let another holiday go by with them being apart. The problem was, Mason was very slow to respond to her advances of friendship. In fact, she could almost say he was reluctant.

Which was unnerving, because the Mason she

knew had been of stalwart heart. He wouldn't change his mind.

She *had* pushed him away pretty hard, though. Mimi sighed and put some cupcakes into the oven. Valentine looked up.

"Something wrong?"

Mimi shook her head. "I've got Jefferson cowboy blues."

Valentine laughed. "I remember having those."

"When do they subside?"

Valentine put a dab of frosting on some gingerbread men. "I'd say about the time you finally hear them say 'I do.'"

Mimi blinked. "I'm in trouble, then. I have no wedding date, and my intended isn't courting these days."

"He's just giving you your space."

Mimi washed her hands. "There's such a thing as too much space."

Valentine laughed. "Miss him, do you?"

"Terribly."

"You'd best get a move on, then," Valentine told her. "I heard there's been quite a throng of admirers hanging around the sheriff's office."

Mimi shook her head. "That's exactly what I

would have done before, try to keep Mason all to myself. My behavior caused all kinds of problems."

Valentine shrugged. "So will letting another woman steal him."

The idea was worrisome, but Mimi pushed it out of her mind. "If it's meant to be, it will be. I've waited so many years for Mason that I'd like to think whatever feelings he has for me aren't biased by jealousy or insecurity."

"Okay," Valentine said, "but just so you know, I heard the Never Lonely Cut-n-Gurls were in town."

Mimi looked up. "I thought Marvella had them all doing charity work now, and they were going to convert the old salon into a home for women in need."

"That's Delilah's old place, which is being rebuilt. Marvella's salon is still open for business." Valentine smiled. "She has it strictly on the level nowadays, but I still don't trust those girls."

Mimi blinked. "I'm not sure I would, either."

"Really?" Valentine put her decorated gingerbread men into the refrigerator to cool. "Given your newfound sense of non-jealousy and non-clingy be-havior, would you care to know that they're paying a visit to Mason's office right now?"

Mimi gulped. That's where she and Mason had first made love! Well, the second time they'd made love, but the first time since she'd been a woman who had just told her man the truth. Years ago, the first time they'd made love, neither of them had understood their feelings. He'd reacted to her father's illness, and she'd allowed him to comfort her.

But the second time marked a special turning point in their relationship. She wasn't going to give anyone else a chance with her man. Mimi yanked off her apron, checked her face for flour, fluffed her hair and dashed out the door without saying another word.

There was only so much good, ladylike behavior she could stomach.

Chapter Eighteen

Mason smiled when Mimi walked into his office. She didn't so much walk as blow right through. Her cheeks were red; her blond hair was somewhat askew. Why, she looked as if she'd run all the way down to his office. Mason chuckled and leaned back in his chair. He put his heels on the desk and silently applauded himself for finally figuring out the right method for teasing his little hell-belle out of her cemented position of "I need time."

He'd given her plenty of time. He was impatient to make her his. But he knew her well, and a man could give a woman too damn much time to make up her mind.

Some minds, like Mimi's, weren't really designed to be made up. At least not without a little incentive.

So when the Never Lonely Cut-n-Gurls walked

into his office, Mason knew he had a sterling opportunity to get his little gal going. He'd stepped outside his office for a moment and called Valentine, asking her if she'd do him the favor of letting her new assistant baker know that company had come to town.

Ah, life was sweet, Mason thought, watching Mimi's back stiffen as she noted a couple of girls draped on his desk and a few others in provocative poses in chairs around his office. Some just leaned against the wall, and that was all they had to do to make the dank, bare walls beautiful.

It was great to be a cowboy, he decided. A cowboy learned patience, and patience was what it took to win the prize.

"Mimi, you remember the Never Lonely Cut-n-Gurls from Lonely Hearts Station?" he asked.

"Yes." She nodded at them, but it was not the world's friendliest nod. "What brings you stylists to town?"

"We decided to visit and see what y'all are doing to make Union Junction such a success," a tall blonde said. "We've been hearing such good things about your town and how it's growing."

"Must be your sheriff," a perky brunette said from her place on Mason's desk.

Mimi blinked. "Have you visited the Union Junction Salon? They're a big part of our growth.

They've had lots of good ideas. And Delilah's been helping out. I'm sure they could tell you what you want to know."

A tiny redhead smiled at her lazily. "We figured the sheriff could tell us everything about his town's demographics."

"Demographics?" Mimi asked. "I don't think so. The town clerk and registrar would know all those things. Her name is Mrs. Fancy, and if you come back when she's in her office, she can tell you about that topic."

"Mimi, don't you want us to talk to the new sheriff and offer him our most sincere congratulations?" the blonde asked.

The other ladies in the room giggled, looking at her sneakily. Mason, the cad, just grinned. *Any moment, I expect him to pull out a cigar and celebrate the glories of being a man with females vying for his attention.*

He winked at her. Mimi glared back. "I don't mind you talking to him," she said sweetly. "I just don't want you doing anything else with him."

The smile on Mason's face grew bigger but Mimi didn't care.

"Why, Mimi," the redhead said, "we weren't aware that you'd staked a claim on Mason."

"I haven't. He staked a claim on *me*."

"I don't see a ring," the brunette said saucily.

Which was true, Mimi decided, and it was also her fault. He'd offered to buy her a ring. Stung, she opened her mouth to tell the brunette to mind her own business.

"Well, you can't see the ring when it's still in the box," Mason said, reaching into his desk to pull out a silver-wrapped box he'd been keeping there ever since he'd followed Mimi up to Hawk's. He'd been hoping and praying that one day this little box would be opened.

Mimi stared at him, her eyes huge. Mason grinned, feeling pretty proud of himself.

"Let us see it, Mason," one of the girls said, but he shook his head.

"Can't, ladies. This is for Mimi's eyes only."

She smiled at him, and in her eyes, he read the answer he'd been waiting for. "You ladies will have to excuse us," he said. "Mimi and I have some things to discuss."

"Sure, Mason." The Never Lonely Cut-n-Gurls rose and went slowly to the door.

"Lucky you," one said on her way out the door.

"Call us if it doesn't work out," another said with a flounce at Mimi as she left.

"Congratulations," three murmured as they walked out.

The room emptied, and Mason closed the door behind them. He put the ring box back into the drawer and looked at Mimi with his most official sheriff expression. "Now, what brings you here, Miss Mimi?"

Her lips parted. "Mason!"

He sat down and waited. "Just a casual hello?"

She fidgeted, and he enjoyed having her on the hot seat for once. Usually, it was him at the mercy of Mimi.

"I heard you had company," she said, "and I felt you'd appreciate a rescue."

"Ah. Coming to my rescue again." He grinned.

"Yes."

"No hair spray?"

"I didn't need a weapon for that crowd," Mimi said disdainfully. "Just my wits."

He smiled. "I'm glad you came to see me."

"So about that box," Mimi said.

"Yes?" He raised his eyebrows, hoping she'd ask more about it. This time, he wanted her to want him—and to show it.

"Is it really for me?"

Nodding, he pulled it back out, sitting it on top of his desk so that she could be tempted by it. "I bought it several months ago."

She took a step forward. Mason grinned. "After I asked your father for your hand in marriage."

Mimi blinked. "You did that?"

"Of course! It's the respectful thing to do. And I do respect you, Mimi."

"He never told me."

"The sheriff is wise beyond his years," Mason said. "He knew you thought you needed time."

"I didn't need as much time as you've given me," Mimi admitted.

"You didn't?" If that was so, he was glad to hear it!

"No. But you quit coming around."

"I see you quite frequently."

"You don't sleep in my bed."

"Oh," he said with a smile. "You miss me."

"I just thought maybe every once in a while…yes, damn it, I miss you."

Grinning, he got up from his chair and carried the box with him. "So, Mimi," he said.

"Yes, Mason?"

He looked into her eyes. "I think after all these years, it's just you and me, babe."

She smiled. "It feels right."

"Let me tell you what I see for our future, and let's see if you agree." He kissed her on the lips, enjoying the feel of her once again connected to him. His heart jumped, telling him that everything was right about this moment. "Lots of kids. Lots of sex. Lots of fun. Years of you making me crazy, and years of me—"

"Making me crazy," she said with a smile. "I like the future you see."

"Big wedding."

"The biggest," she said. "We have a lot of friends who are going to be happy for us."

"No more ghosts from the past for either of us," Mason said. "We want a clean closet for our children. No skeletons, just fresh Cannady-Jefferson memories."

"That sounds wonderful."

He kissed her again, delighted by the happiness he saw in her eyes. "Do you want to make love to me first, or open this box?"

She giggled. "Mason, you're crazy. Of course I want the box first!"

He laughed. "I was hoping you'd say that. I spent three hours in the store designing this ring."

Mimi's eyes grew wide. "You did?"

"Yes. But Nanette needs to go with us to help pick out wedding bands."

"Oh, she'll love that." Mimi glowed, and he knew he was doing everything right.

"So, Mimi Cannady," he said, getting down on one knee. "I've loved you for years. I loved you before I even knew what true love was. I couldn't even imagine being in love, and somehow, you showed me how much those feelings would mean to me." He watched as Mimi's eyes teared a little, and he smiled. "I do love you, girl. You're the only woman I've ever loved."

Mimi held his hand tightly. It felt very much as if they were saying their wedding vows now, Mason realized. "So I'm asking you to accept this ring, and marry me, and be at my side forever," he said, giving her the box.

She took it from him, and he felt her tremble just the slightest bit as she looked at him. Then, in typical Mimi fashion, she tore the wrapping off and pulled the box open. "Oh, Mason," she said, "I've never seen anything like it."

He grinned, feeling he'd designed a ring for a queen. She was his queen. His rodeo queen, his queen of hearts and the queen of his life. "Three curving rows of diamonds, and then one big fat one in the center, heart shaped, of course, to show you that I know that what we have is special. It's one of a kind."

Mimi started to cry as he slipped the ring on her finger. She flung her arms around his neck and kissed him as he'd never been kissed before. Mason knew in that moment he had found the love his father had wanted all his boys to know. Grateful tears squeezed at the corners of his eyes as he held Mimi tight. But he didn't really cry, because he was too happy about finally having his Mimi.

Together they walked out onto the streets of Union Junction to tell all their friends and family the good news: Union Junction was going to have the wedding they'd all been waiting for.

The best things in life, of course, were worth the wait.

Chapter Nineteen

It took a couple of months to plan a big Christmas wedding, but Mimi and Mason made good use of the time. When the wedding day dawned, it was clear and lit with sun. Mimi's best friend, Julia Finehurst, had done a marvelous job of coordinating the lavish event, and Mimi wondered if perhaps Julia needed to add wedding planning to her Honey-Do Agency services. The wedding was unlike any Union Junction had ever seen, and a wonderful tribute to two people who had finally found each other.

Each and every Jefferson child participated, which meant that every girl got to be a tiny flower girl and every boy got to bear a small pillow to the altar. Only one pillow held the rings, of course, but the other children didn't care. Every Jefferson brother was a best man, and Mimi, who had grown up with no sisters, had twenty bridesmaids, all stylists from Union Junction and Lonely Hearts Station. Helga was her matron of honor, however, because if she'd had a second mother, Helga would have been her choice.

The wedding was held on the lawns of Malfunction Junction, and the entire town turned out to enjoy it, despite the cold December weather. The best part, though, besides having all their friends and family with them, was her groom. Mimi looked at Mason, admiring him in his wedding attire. A tux with short tails, bolero, dress boots, Western hat—he looked as if he'd stepped out of a movie. And maybe that was appropriate, Mimi thought with a smile.

"What is my bride grinning about?" Mason demanded. "We haven't even said 'I do' yet."

"Everything about you makes me smile," Mimi said. "I love you, Mason."

"I know," he said, in that arrogant tone she was beginning to love. "But you can never love me as much as I do you." He kissed her soundly just to prove that he wasn't completely chauvinistic, and Mimi adored him for being exactly the man she'd always wanted.

"So, I've got a wedding gift for you," Mason said,

returning her to earth. "But you don't get it until after the ceremony."

She smiled. "And I have a wedding gift for you, but you don't get it until after the ceremony, either."

"Is it the pretty nightie?" Mason asked hopefully. "I've been dreaming about it."

"No. It's much better, Mr. Jefferson."

"*Nothing* is better than a naked Mimi."

By now she should be used to blushing, but Mason kept surprising her with his passion.

"Are you sure you want to do this?" he asked.

Mimi gasped. "Get married?" Was he having second thoughts?

Mason laughed and picked her up in his arms. "This huge shindig. My trusty steed is parked over there. We could make a fast getaway and elope. Which means we get down to the goodies faster."

"No," she said, leaning against his chest and enjoying the strong, broad feel of her sheriff. "We'd be dragged back by our own wedding guests. Although I greatly appreciate the fantasy."

"Mmm. However, once I get you alone—"

Mimi kissed him. "That's to tide you over."

Mason smacked his lips. "I think that'll work."

"All right," Last said, coming to get his brother. "If we don't do this thing, you two may not make it to the altar. And there are some of us around here who have odds riding on whether you elope, change your mind or simply keep making us crazy."

Mason frowned. "Who's the bookie?"

"Not telling," Last said, "but I think it might be Nanette."

Mimi and Mason gasped.

"Nah, I'm teasing," Last said. "No one's taking bets. The house would win, because we all know you're going to get married and love it. You deserve it, you stubborn ol' man." He gave his eldest brother a righteous slap on the back.

Mason tried to work up a glare, but Mimi dragged him toward the altar before he could get sidetracked.

Hawk was performing the nontraditional part of the service for them, and they had the pastor to perform traditional vows.

"I like it," Mason said. "I like the fact that you intend to have me wed from all angles. It shows your commitment, my flighty little bride."

He handed her off to Sheriff Cannady with one last hot kiss. "Sorry, Sheriff," he said. "I'm just crazy about your daughter."

"Come on, Mimi," Sheriff Cannady said with a grin. "Let's let Mason off the hook. I can tell he's just itching to become a groom. Which is something I never thought I'd say, and it's going to feel so good to watch it happen."

Mason grinned at her as she walked away with her father. "Hurry, Mimi. Don't make me wait long."

Mimi smiled at him. "You have no idea how long I've waited to hear you say that."

"And I intend to make up for lost time."

Her father tugged her away. "C'mon, girl. Let's get that veil on. Your groom reminds me of some stallions I've owned. Ready and raring to go."

"Dad," Mimi said, laughing. "I'm having so much fun being wooed and wed."

He patted her arm. "You deserve it, Mimi. And heaven only knows, when it finally happens, I'm going to be swilling champagne out of that fountain Julia set up."

They walked into the foyer of the home, which she would now share with Mason. She had always dreamed of living here, part of a big family. Mimi smiled as Julia walked over with her veil. "It's beautiful, Julia. Thank you for everything you've done."

Julia smiled and gently set the long veil over Mimi's golden hair. "You're beautiful. Mason's going to sweep you up and carry you off."

"No, he won't," Mimi said with a laugh, "because Jellyfish is driving the wagon, and he'd be mad if he didn't get to do his part of chauffeuring us out of here."

Julia nodded. "Well, here comes the bride. In the next five minutes, you'll be Mrs. Mimi Jefferson."

Happy tears jumped into Mimi's eyes. "Walk with me."

With her father and her best friend, Mimi walked outside. Her beautiful gown twinkled in the sunlight, which took the chill off the day and gave everything a special glow. Mimi smiled as she took her place behind the procession of bridesmaids, flower girls and ring bearers. The guests, seated in white wicker chairs, rose as lilting strains of the wedding march began to play.

Mason, standing tall at the gazebo altar Julia had concocted, didn't smile at Mimi. He watched her walk down the aisle on her father's arm, on petals of roses the little girls tossed with great importance. She felt herself tremble as Mason's gaze never left hers. It was as if she'd waited all her life to take this walk into his life, and nothing else would ever feel quite like it.

He took her hand and helped her to stand next to him. Her father kissed her, and Mason nodded his thanks to the sheriff for giving him his heart's desire.

It was, Mason decided, as he took Mimi's and Nanette's hands in his, the happiest day of his life.

MANY HOURS LATER, after the last shrimp had been eaten and the wedding guests' feet literally ached from dancing, Mason loaded his new family into the wagon driven by Jellyfish. Sunflower seeds were thrown at them by well-wishers, and they waved goodbye as they moved forward on the journey to the rest of their lives.

Mason held Mimi as she relaxed against him, enjoying the rocking of the wagon as it swayed down the lane. Mason's truck was hidden in a grove just off the lane so no one could decorate it. They planned to make a mad dash into Dallas for an overnight pre-honeymoon. When the holidays were past and the family gone, he and Mimi were taking a two-week honeymoon in Hawaii with Nanette, and he was very much looking forward to having his family all to himself.

When they got to the end of the lane, Mason said, "Thank you for marrying me, Mimi. You've made me happy beyond anything I can say."

She smiled at him, and it went straight into Mason's heart. Now he had what his father had known: a soul mate.

"This is for you," Mason said, and pointed to the sign that arched over the drive to the ranch. Big, scrolling letters read *The Double M,* and Mimi squealed with happiness, feeling one hundred percent part of the family. Which she knew had been Mason's intention, and he was a prince to know exactly what would make her heart happy.

"And this is for you," she said, "a surprise groom's garter."

Mason's eyes lit up. "Shouldn't I wait until we're alone?"

Mimi laughed. "No. This one is G-rated. And a little goofy, but I wanted to make it memorable." Pulling the garter off, she handed it to him.

He was grinning until he saw what adorned the scrap of satin. Mimi had attached a pregnancy stick to the lace—and the tip of the stick was blue.

"Congratulations," Mimi said, "you're a dad. Again."

Mason's heart swelled as he looked at Mimi, his best friend for always. Somehow, *you're a dad—again* were the sweetest words he'd ever heard besides *I do.* He couldn't wait to hear them over and over again through the years.

"Nanette's going to have the first of many brothers and sisters to come. Lucky them to have such a special big sister."

Mimi's eyes twinkled. "We're repeating a Jefferson family tradition. This one's better than the Curse of the Broken Body Parts."

He raised an eyebrow at her.

"Twins," Mimi said.

Holding his girl tightly to him as the wagon moved forward, Mason laughed out loud with joy.

Epilogue

The twelve Jefferson brothers sat around the den of the main house, each trying not to be uncomfortable. It was the day after Christmas, so the tree was pretty but the room had toys and presents scattered everywhere. Fanciful stockings for each and every person lined the stairwell, which was becoming more crowded every year.

The wives and children had all gone into the city to hit the after-holiday sales. Mimi had hired Shoeshine Johnson to chauffeur them in his school bus so they could all ride together, making a party of it. Shoeshine had festooned his bus with garlands, big fat red bows swinging from the garlands and a wreath on the grille. The kids had been delighted, and the men felt good about not having to spend the day in the malls fighting the traffic and elbowing customers.

Although anything would have been better than this, Mason decided. Now that the moment had come, he really didn't want to face it. *Coward,* he told himself, which was only partially true.

He had sought the answers to what had happened to Maverick Jefferson for years. Diligently. Hiring Hawk and Jellyfish had pretty much assured that he would find some answers. He just hadn't expected to have the answers in the black pencil of his father's handwriting.

He felt strangely as if his father's ghost were in the room, and tears pricked at the back of his eyes. "It's now or never," he said. "Who's going to read it?"

"You are," everyone said.

They weren't so much shifting responsibility to him as acknowledging his place as the eldest, Mason knew, and also acknowledging the fact that he'd spent a lot of time and effort worrying about their father over the years. The worst thing, he supposed, would be to find out his father had gone on and led a completely happy life without them. On the other hand, Mason desperately hoped his father had been happy and well.

He nodded. "All right," he said, reaching out with somewhat unsteady hands to pick up the book. "Here we go."

Slowly, he opened the book, careful not to crack

the well-weathered spine. Then he began to read aloud from the pages, pronouncing each word carefully.

"August 1. Washington State. Not really sure what I'm doing here."

Mason looked up. "He doesn't date the year."
Last waved a hand. "Go on."
"It skips to August 15," Mason said.

"Northern California. Miss Alaska. Not sure why. Froze my ass off there."

The men chuckled.
Mason took a deep breath.

"Sept. 1. Heading back to Alaska. Like the cold the best. Don't feel anything when the weather forces survival on a person.

"Oct. 1. Feel vaguely like I left something important behind. Not sure where. Think my boys are going to call me today."

Mason's hands started to tremble, and he heard Crockett sigh. He forced himself to read on.

"Oct. 20. Feel really cold. I know I used to live in a really hot place, but I can't remember where. Am living with some fishermen. They take me out with them to do some ice-hole fishing. Sometimes we go by boat. The world is really pretty out there. There's nothing for miles but wild, raw beauty. The feeling of being alone is somehow what I deserve."

Fannin made a sound that could have been a curse word. Navarro leaned back, putting his boots on the table. The clock on the mantel ticked, which Mason usually found comforting. But not today. It reminded him of the moments of his father's life that had ticked away, with him being clearly somewhat confused. Having recently suffered a head injury himself and feeling vaguely out of line with the rest of his body occasionally, he knew his father had been searching for who he was, not what he didn't have.

The knowledge made his heart heal in slow, soothing waves. "He was sick," Mason said. "I wonder if he'd hit his head on something while he was out working and got confused. I don't think he would have left us had he not suffered some type of injury."

"Could have been internal," Bandera said. "A small stroke or something. I know he'd always missed Mom, but he doesn't talk about it in the journal. Unless you haven't gotten there."

"Well," Mason said, "he was trying to remember a lot about his life. For example, there's a list of his favorite foods in here. There's a list of what he'd eaten recently. And," he said, turning to the last page, "there's a family tree with all our birth names." He smiled. "He's got Mom's name surrounded by a heart. There are side notes in a different section about her. For example, he writes,

'I was sure as hell no hero. I don't know why she loved me. But she did, and I loved her for it, with all the love a man can give anyone.'"

"Not surprised by that," Frisco Joe said. "He was a one-woman man."

"And a one-family man," Laredo said.

"Now here's something strange," Mason said. "On the back of the family tree, he's written some history in a sort of journalistic style, without dates."

"Read it," Tex said. "The suspense is killing me."

Mason glared at him for a second, then his gaze returned to his father's writing.

"My great-grandparents were hardworking people from Europe who settled in Texas and expected life to be hard at the Union Junction ranch, but that was the price of freedom they were willing to pay. They had one child, who married a woman who could take life on the isolated frontier.

"This couple, my parents, had three children: Moira, Maverick and Maximilian, to whom they wanted to leave the ranch. Our parents died unexpectedly. All of us were separated and sent into the foster care system, such as it was at the time. We never saw each other again, and I never got over that. As old as I am, I still remember my brother and sister being taken from me. I couldn't do a damn thing about it. They cried and cried my name, and these days, I hear that sound a lot.

"When I was fourteen I struck out for Texas to take back the family homestead. I thought if I took over the ranch, I could have my brother and sister back. I took our dilapidated house and built it back up with my own two hands. My reputation became one of a man who could eke out a living on the hard dry plains, but the truth was I became hard.

"I never located my brother and sister. The orphanage burned down, and all paperwork was gone, but I don't think anyone who worked there really cared. They didn't remember any of us.

"I never forgot the loneliness. After being in a system that didn't want me, one that carelessly separated families, I longed for a big family of my own. So I married Mercy, because in her I sensed an angel.

"She gave me twelve children, each one of whom I loved with all my soul. They gave me back my heart.

"One day, we'll all be together again."

"Damn it," Ranger said, wiping at his eyes. "I feel sorry for Dad."

"Yeah," Archer said. "Wonder why he never told us about his brother and sister."

"He couldn't," Mason said, finally understanding his father after all these years. "He couldn't save them, so he locked it away inside him. It was too painful."

"He put all his love and efforts into us," Frisco Joe said. "We had the benefit of him home-schooling us with what he'd learned from his immigrant parents, and he forged our family and taught us to rely on each other."

They looked around in the Christmas-lit room, the house they now knew their great-grandparents had built and had struggled to keep and which their father had fought to take back. Then they all went outside to look at the wide, vast land, which was their birthright.

Then they looked at the sky, silently thanking their father for giving them everything he had and for making them the men they had become.

There was no greater love.

Turn the page for a sneak peek
at a special new miniseries,
THE TULIPS SALOON,
by Tina Leonard,
coming September 2006 only from
Harlequin American Romance.

You may remember
the ladies of Tulips, Texas, from
CROCKETT'S SEDUCTION *of the* COWBOYS
BY THE DOZEN *miniseries. Tulips is run by*
women,
and their goal is to grow the small town.
To do this, they must band together
and guide the men.
Read about their first (willing!) victim, Sheriff
Duke Forrester, in
MY BABY, MY BRIDE.

It was Ladies Only Day in the Tulips Saloon in Tulips, Texas, but Sheriff Duke Forrester pitched the heavy glass-and-wood doors open anyway, drawing a gasp from the crowd of women clustered in the center of the saloon.

The ladies were, as usual, hiding something from him. In this town named by women and mostly run by women—it was true that behind every good woman there was a woman who'd taught her everything she knew—he had learned to outmaneuver both the young and older population of ladies bent on intrigues of the social, sexual and secretive varieties.

"I heard," he said, his voice a no-nonsense drawl, "that Liberty Wentworth was back in town. You ladies wouldn't know anything about that, would you?"

They shook their heads and tightened their circle. It was, he decided, almost an engraved invitation for him to storm their protective clutch and find out what they were up to. By now, they should know he was on to them. Duke grinned, edging a foot closer to the ladies. Their faces became darling with round-eyed concern.

"Now, this is Ladies Only Day," Helen Granger said sternly. "Sheriff, you know that means no gentlemen in here."

"Considering there are, what, maybe ten men in this town of fifty residents, I have to take exception to the rule. I think you ladies just like having one day when you know I won't be allowed in."

"Is one day of sisterhood too much to ask?" Helen demanded. "One day of female bonding in our saloon? Hen talk can't interest you that much, Sheriff."

The hen talk comment gave them away, Duke decided, nearly drooling to see what they were hiding. Women never called their chatter hen talk, and if a man called it that, he'd probably lose his hat from the gale wind force of them yelling it off his head. "All right, ladies," he said, gently moving Pansy to one side. "Let's see what you're up to this time."

Of course, after he'd parted the women, he would always look back and remember that he'd wished he hadn't. Because there in the center of the sheltering circle of her friends was Liberty Wentworth, the blond bombshell who had detonated his heart, still possessing the face of an angel and wearing the white wedding gown of his never-ending fantasies.

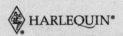

HARLEQUIN®

American ROMANCE®

To Wed, or Not To Wed

A new series about love, relationships and the road to the altar

THE MAN SHE'LL MARRY
by Ann Roth

Cinnamon Smith's attraction to
Nick Mahoney is purely physical—
or so she thinks. From the moment
she meets him, Cinnamon can't seem
to get him out of her mind, even though
Nick is miles from her idea of the
right man for her. But finding love—
and the right man to marry—
rarely happens as we expect!

Available June, whereever books are sold.

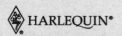

HARLEQUIN®

American ROMANCE®

A THREE-BOOK SERIES BY

Kaitlyn Rice

Heartland Sisters

To the folks in Augusta, Kansas, the three sisters
were the Blume girls—a little pitiable, a bit mysterious
and different enough to be feared.

The three sisters may have received an odd upbringing,
but there's nothing odd about the affection, esteem
and support they have for one another, no matter
what the crises that come their way.

THE THIRD DAUGHTER'S WISH

When Josie Blume starts to search for the father she's
never known, she's trying to lay some family ghosts to rest.
Other surprises are in store on her journey back into time—
and one of them is rediscovering Gabe Thomas, a man who
shares not only her past and present but her future, too.

Available June 2006

Also look for:

THE LATE BLOOMER'S BABY
Available October 2005

THE RUNAWAY BRIDESMAID
Available February 2006

Available wherever Harlequin books are sold.

Home improvement has never seen results like this!

When she receives a large inheritance,
Stacy Sommers decides she is finally going
to update her kitchen. Her busy husband has
never wanted to invest in a renovation, but now
has no choice. When the walls come down,
things start to change in ways that neither
of them ever expected.

Finding Home

by Marie Ferrarella

HARLEQUIN®
Next™

HN45
Available June 2006
TheNextNovel.com

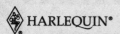

HARLEQUIN®

American ROMANCE®

IS DELIGHTED TO BRING YOU FOUR BOOKS IN A MINIERIES BY POPULAR AUTHOR

Jacqueline Diamond

Downhome Doctors

First-rate doctors
in a town of second chances

DAD BY DEFAULT
On sale June 2006

In Dr. Connor Hardison's view, unwed mothers—and that includes his lovely nurse—aren't responsible enough to raise children. Until the death of a former girlfriend unexpectedly makes him a single father with a four-year-old son. And makes him question his prejudices, too…

Also look for:

THE POLICE CHIEF'S LADY
On sale December 2005

NINE-MONTH SURPRISE
On sale February 2006

A FAMILY AT LAST
On sale April 2006

Available wherever Harlequin books are sold.

If you enjoyed what you just read,
then we've got an offer you can't resist!

Take 2 bestselling love stories FREE!

Plus get a FREE surprise gift!

Clip this page and mail it to Harlequin Reader Service®

IN U.S.A.	IN CANADA
3010 Walden Ave.	P.O. Box 609
P.O. Box 1867	Fort Erie, Ontario
Buffalo, N.Y. 14240-1867	L2A 5X3

YES! Please send me 2 free Harlequin American Romance® novels and my free surprise gift. After receiving them, if I don't wish to receive anymore, I can return the shipping statement marked cancel. If I don't cancel, I will receive 4 brand-new novels every month, before they're available in stores! In the U.S.A., bill me at the bargain price of $4.24 plus 25¢ shipping & handling per book and applicable sales tax, if any*. In Canada, bill me at the bargain price of $4.99 plus 25¢ shipping & handling per book and applicable taxes**. That's the complete price and a savings of at least 10% off the cover prices—what a great deal! I understand that accepting the 2 free books and gift places me under no obligation ever to buy any books. I can always return a shipment and cancel at any time. Even if I never buy another book from Harlequin, the 2 free books and gift are mine to keep forever.

154 HDN DZ7S
354 HDN DZ7T

Name	(PLEASE PRINT)	
Address	Apt.#	
City	State/Prov.	Zip/Postal Code

Not valid to current Harlequin American Romance® subscribers.

Want to try two free books from another series?
Call 1-800-873-8635 or visit www.morefreebooks.com.

* Terms and prices subject to change without notice. Sales tax applicable in N.Y.
** Canadian residents will be charged applicable provincial taxes and GST.
All orders subject to approval. Offer limited to one per household.
® are registered trademarks owned and used by the trademark owner and or its licensee.

AMER04R   ©2004 Harlequin Enterprises Limited

SPECIAL PRICE!

This riveting new saga begins with

In the Dark

by national bestselling author

JUDITH ARNOLD

The party at Hotel Marchand is in full swing when the lights suddenly go out. What does head of security Mac Jensen do first? He's torn between two jobs—protecting the guests at the hotel and keeping the woman he loves safe.

A woman to protect. A hotel to secure. And no idea who's determined to harm them.

On Sale June 2006

HOTEL MARCHAND

**Four sisters.
A family legacy.
And someone is out to destroy it.**

A captivating new limited continuity, launching June 2006

The most beautiful hotel in New Orleans,
and someone is out to destroy it. But mystery,
danger and some surprising family revelations
and discoveries won't stop the Marchand sisters
from protecting their birthright…
and finding love along the way.